I0682294

# The Vortex

## *Visions of Dystopia*

### Science Fiction
### Short Story Collection

*by*
## *Lily Splane*

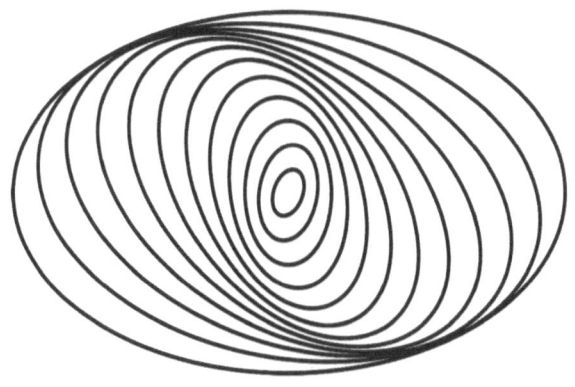

 **Anaphase Publishing**
A Division & Imprint of CYBERLEPSY MEDIA

# The Vortex
*Visions of Dystopia*

*Science Fiction Short Story Collection*

*by*
*Lily Splane*

Copyright © 1986–2002 Lily Splane

ISBN 10: 0-945962-18-5

ISBN 13: 978-0-945962-18-2

Also available in Kindle edition:
ISBN: 978-0-945962-43-4

No part of this work may be reproduced in any form—existing or to be developed in the future—without the express written permission of the author/publisher.

Published in the United States of America

*Anaphase Publishing*
A Division & Imprint of Cyberlepsy Media
4669 Cherokee Avenue, Suite E
San Diego, CA 92116-3654
WWW.CYBERLEPSY.COM

# Contents

# SUNDAY AFTERNOON AT THE MALL

You saw them and you didn't tell anybody? Christ, how could you keep something like that to yourself for so long? I don't blame you for not telling what you did, but you could've omitted that part.

You remember—you skulked around, ducking behind parked cars as you watched those long tan legs emerge from the red Maserati, and oh, if that wasn't enough to die happy with, next came those firm thighs and narrow, compact hips, that wasp waist, those unbelievably huge, erect breasts. Wow! What a figure! And then don't you remember how your excitement shattered to a thousand dirty pieces when he stepped out after her—an Adonis in his own right, muscled and styled and polished.

But life isn't always fair, is it?

And to add insult to injury, she smiled lovingly at him, hooking her arm around his, her hips swaying, brushing sensuously against his as they walked through the parking lot and through the main entrance.

You followed them, you sneaky bastard.

After they bought tickets at the cinema, you rushed to the window and asked the pimple-faced nerd there which movie the previous couple had purchased tickets for, gulped when you heard the answer, and bought a ticket for the same movie: a revival of *The Texas Chainsaw Massacre.*

In the dark you sat behind them, simultaneously entranced by how the woman's golden hair seemed to absolutely glow in the dim light, and irritated at how her head blocked your view. Not that you were interested in the movie at all. That's not what you were there for, you scoundrel.

Through the butchery, the gore, the screams, the whining chainsaw, you became entranced with her voice as she made comments on the film. The words danced in the air like glitter. You didn't stop to consider the content of what she said until after the film. A comment like "Wasn't it creative how Leatherface cut up all the people and they stayed dead?" didn't strike you as particularly profound. Perhaps only stupid. Stupidity in a goddess can be overlooked, can't it? Sure. The man with her knew how to handle it. He had the right idea. He answered, "I'm a little disappointed they didn't switch all the heads on the bodies." The goddess laughed. Clever, that man. You'd never be able to think of things like that. You'd never have a chance with her, you lecherous moron.

Undefeated, you followed them, cautiously, into the pizza joint and sat down at a table just across from them, your face buried in a menu, your eyes dancing at the rim of the menu as you longed for her, ached for the touch of those long manicured fingertips. You ordered wine. You had to.

It didn't even strike you as odd that their pizza was brought to their table in a take-out box. Maybe they were light eaters, you thought. They'd take the rest home.

If you hadn't been so enraptured by her full, glossy lips, her delicate tongue and tiny white teeth, if you hadn't been imaging her mouth all over you, you would have noticed how she chewed. Ferociously, with great difficulty. She was eating the cardboard box, after all. But you didn't see that. You just saw her mouth, the mouth that held the promise of all the erotic fantasies you've ever entertained. And were you unconscious when she said, delicately picking cardboard out of her teeth, "Just like homemade"?

Giving no thought to the entire uneaten pizza they left, you stood behind a tall display case of jade figurines in the jewelry store, watching her, her eyes asparkle, her tongue flicking lightly over those full pink lips as she perused the jewelry cases. Finally she decides on a pair of amethyst earrings and asks the clerk to remove them from the display case. She unscrews the keeps from the earring posts. Her man stands by, smiling approvingly as she brushes back her hair, exposing her ears.

The clerk faints. Didn't you wonder why, for chrissakes? Didn't you wonder why the clerk, when he finally came to, recommended a plastic surgeon? A plastic surgeon, for chrissakes! For that goddess!

The woman seemed bored, preoccupied with other thoughts while you watched her waiting for her man to get measured for a new pair of slacks. When the tailor measured the inseam, you could see the blood drain out of his face, staggering backwards. He stammered and politely asked to be excused.

That should have tipped you off right there. But instead you decided to follow them into Radio Shack. Haven't you tortured yourself enough?

A bizarre sense of humor, you say. It was more than that. No one in their right mind goes into an electronics store and dances in front of the display stereo...when it isn't even turned on. Give it up, relinquish the fantasy before you succumb to it. But would you listen?

Even when you followed them into the shoe store and the woman tried on pair after pair of sandals, rejecting them all because her heels wouldn't touch the floor, you persisted in your fascination with this woman.

You couldn't take your eyes off the long legs, the tiny feet, still shod in high-heels. Her feet must kill her, you lamented. But it made her walk with a sway that brought tears to your eyes. And that's what counts, isn't it?

You relaxed some when they decided to have a little fun in Nurseryland. How amused, how delighted you were, watching as the woman barked commands, shook her finger. "Roll over," she said over and over again at the Chia-pets. You laughed out loud, catching yourself just in time to avoid a collective stare.

Doesn't that bother you?

It was getting late, and the couple decided to stop at one last store on their way out of the mall. You shouldn't have gone in. You shouldn't have followed them. I warned you, I tried to protect you from your own lust, from the perversity of her act. But you had to see, concealed as you were by the display of Venetian blinds. You got a real good look at her, too, when she popped the lid off that can of light blue latex and dipped a finger in it, smearing a stripe across her upper lid.

I told you weren't going to like it. I told you not to look.

Near the exit to the parking lot, dazed, you sat on a bench watching her study a bikini on a mannequin in a display window. She wanted that bikini, you could tell. But there was some reservation in her voice; you caught that. Did her perfect boyfriend or husband or whatever he was to her, refuse to pay for it? The lout! Is that what you heard? Are you sure? You saw him suddenly rush off and dash into an auto supply store just before they locked it up for the night, leaving her alone. The bum, the scumbag. How could he just leave her like that? Surely the bikini was no match in cost for the earrings this beauty never got. You wanted to go up to her, offer to buy the bikini for her, offer to love her forever, be the father of her children. What stopped you?

You knew you didn't have a chance, you loser.

As if struck by lightening, she shot into the swimwear store and returned with the bottom half of the bikini on display, nearly running headlong into her man, who clutched a bag beneath his armpit. He beamed at her, caressed her cheek, pulled something black and leather from the bag. He wrapped the bra of a '75 Corvette around her bust. She giggled in delight. It fit perfectly.

Something dangerous was beginning to eat away at you, by then. It gnawed, and nibbled and clawed at your insides like a starved vulture, waiting to devour your resolve, the last of your good sense.

You followed the couple through the parking lot in the waning light, your presence unnoticed, your heart galloping wildly. You were just two cars away when they got in their Maserati—first the woman, then the man. It was now or never.

You lunged at the passenger side, yanking the door open, the man staring up at you in the dimming light. You grabbed his lapels and pulled him from the car. He didn't struggle. Did you expect he would? Then you grasped him at the sides of the head and jerked. It popped free, just as you'd hoped. You bowled the head into the back seat and thrust the headless body over the seat and onto the floor behind the passenger seat.

"Ken!" the woman screamed.

"Don't worry about that asshole. It's you and me from now on baby!"

What? Me? Hell, who'd believe me?

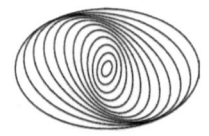

# CONVERGENCE

I am vaguely aware that what I am now experiencing is not what it seems to be, or more precisely, is not all there seems to be.

Sometimes, I don't know how I know what I know.

I am religious by no means, but there is something....

A disturbing feeling, a longing gnaws at my insides, begging to be recognized.

It is an ancient craving, a want....

The animals know it, feel it, acknowledge it without feeling obligated to worship it.

I am an atheist, on the brink of death. I reach out to something infinite, larger than life itself.

In animal echoes, I feel and hear references to the "really big thing" and I understand.

The low hum of the churning water in the life-support reservoirs resonated relentlessly throughout the spacious quarantine area. Lieutenant Maxine Sparks gazed at the acoustic ceiling, then jerked her head from the padded supports to study the white emptiness of the space station medical confinement area. The bright lighting smarted her eyes as she half-consciously looked down the walls and across to her own monitoring equipment. The morphine analog drip monitor softly signaled each drop falling into her vein. These things would be the last things she would ever see, now that the terminal status of her injuries had been confirmed. Maxine secretly thanked someone, or something nameless, that she would not have to experience the cruelty of her own natural pain chemistry. A tear of desolation and hopelessness escaped down her calm, expressionless face.

* * *

Shir'h writhed and groaned, clutching the animal skins beneath her tightly, fighting to maintain the consciousness she knew was leaving her bit by bit. The medicine woman weaved and wailed over her, inducing family and tribe members to join efforts in chasing the pain demons from inside her. The several small fires in the cave threw mischievous shadows into a frantic animal-like dance on the rocky walls. Friend Lala wiped the sweat from Shir'h's forehead. Shir'h's mate stroked her hands and arms, joining in the medicine woman's chant to abolish the pain spirits from her blood. She felt a smile blossom on her pain-anguished face as a tear dove down her cheek.

Maxine lay motionless, empty, sensationless, remembering the random burst of the propulsion tank that had slammed her body noiselessly against the outer hull of the space station during a routine EVA. The medics responded efficiently, emotionlessly to her pleas for extrication from the vacuum of space before the integrity of her suit could fail.

Automatically, mindlessly, they had pulled her into the external airlock and quickly inflated the medical pressure suit around her torso and legs. But it was too late; the searing pain from her crushed spine had diminished to a fiery tingle that descended and jab-danced down the nerve tracks of her legs. In minutes, following a flurry of bone scans and private whispers, the team of experts had concluded that Maxine's injuries were inoperable; death was imminent. Morphine analogs flowed generously into her and she was shunted into isolation. News of her accident and impending demise would be kept from the rest of the crew to prevent any incident of space panic.

\* \* \*

Shir'h's fall from the cliff had not been an unusual accident within the tribe; many had fallen during the forced stampeding of the animals. Her screams had brought not only members of her own tribe, but also wanderers from a neighboring community. Cleansing and binding had begun immediately. Young women pulled twigs and gouged pebbles from the flesh in her back. Young boys wrapped Shir'h in a hide litter to pull her as comfortably as possible back to her family's dwelling.

She remembered crying from the excruciating pain and greeting the buzzing blackness several times before meeting her mate's shocked gaze at the cave's entrance. He had abandoned his carving of the large animal carcass; others also had stopped their chores as the cave walls repelled Shir'h's cries.

\* \* \*

Devoid of the barbaric pain and suffering of millennia past, Maxine was left completely alone with the thoughts of her own death, the incessant beep of the morphine drip, and the wheeze of the respirator, counting, measuring—tallying her last breaths. Had she wanted to speak, been able to, there would be no one there to hear her; it was against regulations. She was alone, more alone than she could ever have believed possible.

No pain, no discomfort. But morphine could not fill the incredible emptiness, the need to look into a compassionate face, the indescribable need to be held—just one last time. The pace of the morphine drip quickened. Maxine's mind swam in the murky swamp of a pharmaceutical stupor.

* * *

To attend to Shir'h, the entire routine of the tribe had been suspended without complaint or question. Throughout the day and into the night, Shir'h's mate, children and tribal kin sang to her, stroked her, bathed her in cool spring water. Other young ones brought furs from their own sleeping places to pack around her broken body. The medicine woman chanted quietly over her, smearing red ochre powder on her face. Flowers and blooming grasses were brought and arranged upon her. Probing fingers pushed small morsels of food into her mouth. She smiled her appreciation and affection to her caregivers. The stabbing pains in her back and legs seemed markedly lessened with each stroke of another's hands, with each swab of a wet square of fur on her forehead, with each soft, heartfelt note sung to her.

* * *

Again the longings, the knowledge of something very important, something infinite, crept into Maxine's thoughts. She had never been more aware of it than now. Almost imperceptibly, it seemed to call to her.

A medic came into the room to read Maxine's vital signs; she could not feel his touch as he grasped her arm to reposition the electropad sensors. He asked if she would like the porthole unshielded. Maxine blinked and nodded.

The huge blackness of space tugged her eyes out into it. Crystal stars beckoned, invited her attention, erased the starkness of medical confinement. The arrangement of the stars traced out patterns and constellations known for eons. She no longer felt empty, or alone.

* * *

Something important will happen. There is more, thought Shir'h. Animal voices from outside screeched and snorted above the soft droning of the attentive, consoling tribe. She whispered a request for the others to move aside. The velvet of the night sky opened to her from the entrance of the cave. *The "really big thing" waits for me,* she thought. The stars twinkled in images of animals seen only in the Wise Ones' imaginations.

* * *

Maxine heard her breathing become irregular as she continued to stare intently out into space. The beep of the morphine drip slowed. No one came. The void of space was her only company; it waited patiently for her, to receive her last recognition of it before it swallowed her limp, lifeless body through pre-programmed jettison.

\* \* \*

A sharp stabbing pain convulsed through Shir'h's body. Giving its unexpectedness little acknowledgement, she continued to stare out into the black dome of night, fixing the constellations in her consciousness, suppressing awareness of the animal sounds and the singing. The great night would accept her unquestioningly, as her family and tribal kin always had.

\* \* \*

*Gushing, buzzing sound in my ears, stars no longer visible in an amorphous darkness. I feel nothing—no body, no emotion. Bizarre, unconnected thoughts monopolize a need to hold on. I am no longer of the family-tribe, but of the universal tribe. I am not an "I." All exists here. Nothingness everywhere. Unlimited potential. Finalized lifetime. Infinity. Termination. Oneness. Isolation. I hear myself babbling as I fall, am pulled through...through life, through consciousness, through time itself.*

"Maksee..." *Why did I say that? What is this word...why...what....*

"Shir..." *What does that mean? I don't understand. I don't...I....*

The Universe implodes, only to start anew.

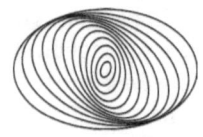

# WITHOUT DARK MATTER...

Uncoiling, unraveling, unclumping, diffusing.
Darkness tears the light asunder, disposing of its hold,
  its brilliant fifteen-billion-year dance.
Dissolution, fragmentation, crumbling worlds.
Decayed dreams, dissolved lives.
Disorder.
Turbulence gone awry.
Chaos out of rhythm.
Disarrangement.
Displaced plans, scattered hopes.
Disintegrated futures, squandered potentials.
Expulsion from the cradle of creation.

Universal evanescence.

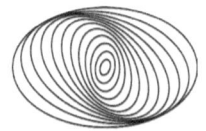

# FEEDBACK LOOP

Accelerating to a panicked trot, Dr. Chelsea Waters threaded her sweating, exhausted body through the sludge of people and news cameras choking the entrance to The Memory Recovery Institute.

"What's going on? What the hell is this?" she shrieked into the crowd as she crammed past the jabbing elbows, intruding microphones and flashing cameras.

"Dr. Waters, we have it on unquestionable authority that you have succeeded in permanently interfacing a human subject with your mainframe computer in the basement," a nondescript reporter said as he offensively shoved a microphone at Chelsea's mouth, clipping her lower lip with it.

"Get away from me, jerk!" Chelsea was livid; air gushed into her tired lungs in measured bursts as her tongue searched for bleeding. "Where did you get this crap?" Just then, another reporter busted through the crowd to confront her.

"Dr. Waters, do you have any comments?"

"NO!" Chelsea weaseled angrily past the last two TV cameras and clearing the security guard, scrambled down the long hall to the Neural Tracing Lab. She squeezed through the door, locking it behind her.

"What the hell's going on out there?" she panted as the entire lab team stared at her in her disheveled and angry condition.

"Someone phoned in anonymously to every major TV and radio station this side of the Rockies, claiming that some nut had breached our security system and had hooked his bean up to the mainframe. The story goes that we can't get him out, and he's threatening to put himself into a feedback loop if we don't erase the memories that we so carefully recovered for him a few years back," Dr. Blalock casually explained.

"It's not true is it? It can't be...." Chelsea gulped as her words trailed off.

In his usual cruel way, Dr. Blalock took his time in replying. He seemed to enjoy hanging others by their heels over a cliff when it came to divulging eagerly awaited answers. "No—no one's been down there since the accident in '84," he finally revealed.

"God, that's all we need...more bad press. It's hard enough to convince the government our research is worthwhile and safe, without more incidents to fog up the importance of it. Somebody's gotta clear those media vultures out before they put that bullshit on the air. Where's Beth?" Chelsea looked around the lab for an answer from any of the staring faces.

Danica Ortega volunteered to find Beth. Use of the intercom during this time would only serve to prompt the news teams to question Beth unprepared if they knew she was within earshot.

Chelsea leaned back into the lab bench, steadying herself with a tight grip on the edge of the table as she tried to regain her composure and a semblance of professionalism. Blonde strands of hair hung in disarray around her moist face. She silently cursed the news media for their unwarranted and frivolous leap on such a wild story—an anonymous tip, at that. News people were the greediest, most desperate creatures on the planet, she decided. All the more reason to despise them: they were the lowest form of humanoid. Except for Beth.

Beth Johnston was perhaps the most competent woman on the team, besides herself. And she was her best friend. What a shame Beth had not been born male. Chelsea reflected on how she often told Beth she wished she could find a man like her. Chelsea loved Beth in a way that she had never loved any man.

Beth's always smiling young face peeked in through the door porthole. Entering the lab, she teased, "Hey, Chelsea, who's the party for?"

"Haven't you heard? The whole damn institute—and we can label it a wake if we don't clear those bastards out pronto." Chelsea took a deep breath, and exhaling slowly, continued. "Some psycho called every TV and radio station in the West and told them there was someone permanently connected via wetware to the mainframe in the basement. The foyer's crawling with every reporter and journalist that can shuffle and hold a mike."

"My God, who would do such a thing? What could they possibly get out of it?" Beth asked in amazement.

"Don't know, Beth. We gotta get 'em out of here. We can't stand the scrutiny—not now."

"O.K., I'll go see what I can do. Wait...why don't you come with me? It'll be very good PR if the head of the team just has the guts to show her face. You can answer some of the more technical questions better than I can." Beth squeezed Chelsea's arm as if trying to push a "yes" button.

"You've got to be kidding! You know I have no tact. That's why they hired *you*. You have a talent for appeasing the creeps without pissing them off."

"Don't worry, Chelsea. I'll clarify anything you say, or I'll answer for you when I can. It'll be O.K. They'll eat it up."

Beth Johnston preceded Dr. Chelsea Waters to the increasingly noisy stampede of eager and demanding reporters. Beth stepped up to the rope divider and in a surprisingly deep and loud voice, commanded the crowd to silence. The herd hushed to a murmur as Beth cleverly and methodically explained how they had been sent on a snipe hunt—yet again. Reporters politely took turns asking their ridiculous questions as Beth fielded them expertly and calmly, one at a time. She droned on about the institute's most mundane research, and Chelsea could sense a cloud of boredom sag into the crowd, dulling it, quieting it, seducing it. The crowd belonged to Beth—it was under her spell. Chelsea had never seen anything like it. Gradually the foyer emptied, leaving a few sparsely placed stragglers who drifted from wall to wall, grasping at their tiny brains for more probing questions to ask, but finally submitting to the defeat of utter tedium.

"Beth, how did you do that? No one got mad, accused us of cover-ups or secret experiments. How could this happen like this?" Chelsea prodded Beth for her secrets.

"Easy—I gave them information—way, way *too much* information. That's not what they wanted, they wanted a confession. Very simple really—if you can't tell them anything, tell them *everything.*"

"Jesus, I hate reporters," Chelsea said. "I'm glad you quit that grind and came to work for us. What would we do without you?"

"Probably cause a national incident," Beth said placing her hand on Chelsea's shoulder as they walked back to the lab.

"It's about time, girls," Dr. Blalock sneered as he watched Beth and Chelsea enter the lab together. "We have four appointments set up for you today—first one is in...ten minutes and forty-one seconds. Get to crackin'. All four have to be finished today. No horsing around." Dr. Blalock's corpulent face remained frozen and expressionless in furrows of authoritarian seriousness. He wheezed audibly as his head tilted and sank his chin into the rubber raft of blubber encircling his neck.

"Girls. Did you hear that?" Chelsea mumbled to Beth. "Son-of-bitch got his doctorate a year after I started work here."

"Easy, Chelsea. He's just jealous of female friendships. They may even scare him a bit. It's his problem, and he can't make it anyone else's if they don't let him."

"The Mussolini of laboratory analysis strikes again!" Chelsea barked in a stifled voice.

A chorus of titters emanated from the rear of the lab as assistants Danica Ortega and Marina Haddad desperately tried to mask their amusement with Chelsea's off-handed comment.

Dr. Blalock interrupted in his deliberate German growl, "O.K., girls. The lab's all yours until 4:00 P.M. I'm off to stratum three."

\* \* \* \*

Danica paged their first subject. "Mr. William Henderson, please present your ID at the security desk." In two minutes, a weathered and morally defeated young man skulked into the lab.

This was Henderson's fifth treatment, and he routinely removed his tattered, filthy shirt and sat in the specially designed chair near the computer console. Danica gently positioned the headband and leads as Chelsea flipped toggle switches and cranked dials in a furious blur of expert certainty.

Chelsea opened Henderson's file folder and began writing a few notes. "How has your therapy been coming along, Will? Are you able to remember more since last week?"

"Uh...I guess. My shrink says I still recall in fragments—nothing seems to be connected or related to anything else. Those memories just don't seem to be a part of my life yet. It's like someone was playing a tape inside my head—like some sort of disjointed avant-garde movie or something," Henderson said in a slow, deliberate drawl.

"You know it's going to take some time before everything falls into place for you—but it will, I promise. Have you been staying off the bottle, Will? The treatments will take longer if you go back to drinking. Wernicke's Encephalopathy is a very serious disease—your brain has been damaged by the alcohol and lack of proper nutrition. Years ago, what we are doing for you here would have been impossible," Chelsea said.

"Yeah...uh, no. No, I'm not boozin', I swear."

"Maybe we can boost the Cerebrine a bit, and add some Zapponin."

"Zappo—what?" Henderson asked in a sleepy, half-witted tone.

"Zapponin. It speeds up the engram 're-etching' process. Cerebrine helps you retrieve those lost chunks of memory, Zapponin speeds up the re-allocation and save stages—kind of like making a better copy of a suspect disk. We'll be re-mapping your engrams so your memories will be more fluid and make better sense to you." Chelsea had to go through this long explanation of the treatment each and every time Henderson came in. His brain was still making faulty memory engrams and the organization of thought was deteriorating almost as fast as memories could be recovered and re-etched. He was a most challenging, but most promising subject. Good results with his treatment could bring in millions in research grants.

Marina Haddad injected the prescribed mixture of drugs into Henderson's carotid artery as Chelsea watched the oscilloscope and the prompt lights on the console. Henderson grinned foolishly, obviously enjoying the exotic beauty of Marina's Lebanese background.

"O.K., Will. Close your eyes. We're going to turn you around. Remember, never try to turn around and look at the screen; it's very dangerous. If you need to stop for any reason, just say so. We'll all be in here with you. Don't worry about a thing, we're professionals and we've seen it all. When the tape is finished, you can take it to your therapist, just like before. Now relax, and let your mind tell you who you are." Chelsea backed away from the console and sat at her desk, still keeping her eyes on Henderson. She couldn't remove her gaze from him for a second; he had on several occasions flung off his blinders and turned around to look at the screen anyway, nearly trapping himself in a feedback loop. Fortunately, his damaged brain took longer to comprehend things and to sync with the images on the screen, avoiding any serious outcome. Chelsea sat, fixed on the images flowing on the huge monitor, still in awe of the technology that could allow a whole roomful of observers to crawl around inside someone's head and watch his or her life in review.

Henderson's muscles began their usual fine twitching, then relaxed into flaccid uselessness as he sat calmly allowing the Cerebrine to coax memories from his brain. The screen behind him filled with vibrant, crystalline pictures. Voices and music spilled out into the room for all but the ear-muffed Henderson to hear.

Ninety minutes passed. As the Zapponin wore off, the images slowed to a sluggish creep. Chelsea removed the earmuffs and spoke to Henderson in a commanding tone, jolting him from his dream-like mind excursion.

"It...it was beautiful. It was fantastic—the best ever. Can I come back tomorrow? Please?" Henderson pleaded. His face took on a pleasant, child-like expression, the wrinkles almost ironing themselves out right before Chelsea's eyes.

"I guess so, Will. I can't see any harm—wait. No, you have to see your therapist first. He has to see this new tape before we proceed. Call me here at the lab when you're ready. Extension 132."

"It was so beautiful. I gotta tell some of my friends," Henderson said.

Chelsea fought to conceal her excitement. More drunks to study—more grants. There was no stopping her now. "Remember, they have to be dry for at least four days before they come in. We can't treat anyone with the DT's. By the way, what made this time so much better for you than the times before?"

"I don't know. It was just more...real. More color, more sound. I swear I could smell things...and the textures...."

"You felt textures? You remembered these?" Chelsea was intrigued with his exacting descriptions and use of different words. It was as if he had a vocabulary transplant.

"Yeah, like they were right under my hand! I felt my bunny, petting my bunny...when I was six—I remember! I actually felt how soft that rabbit was. I haven't even seen a rabbit in ten years, not since before I started to drink. I don't remember doing anything before I started drinking, and now...I remember I was six and had a pet rabbit... and it's *my* memory—I know it," Henderson said as he put his shirt back on and walked dreamily out the door.

"How odd. He's never remembered anything during the treatment before. It always took a session with his therapist watching the tape with him to get him to put it all together," Chelsea remarked.

Chelsea motioned to Danica to page the next patient. An almost gaunt elderly lady entered the lab, nervously scanning the equipment and the console. She had never undergone the treatment and had many questions. Patiently, Chelsea explained the procedure step by step, then spent a few silent moments reading the lady's medical history.

She discovered the lady had been in an automobile accident several years ago. Her memory of it had been so completely suppressed that she believed her husband was still alive and would be returning to her any day. She could not tell anyone how long he had been gone or even where he was. All she knew was that she had to wait for him. And wait she did—every evening at a dinner table set for two, sitting in a new dress she had purchased that afternoon, staring out the screen door onto the brilliantly lighted front porch—every night for nineteen years.

"Danica, look at this. Get Dr. Blalock, this is going to be a rough one," Chelsea said.

"How sad. Can't you just leave her be? Who's she hurting?"

"Apparently she isn't eating but once a day—she's lost fifty-six pounds. She buys a new dress every day—Jesus where does she put them all? Her family can't afford to pay her electric bill anymore—they sent her to a therapist. No luck. He sent her here. We'll need a sedative, get clearance for that as well."

Doctor Blalock returned with Danica and a syringe full of a mild hypnotic. "No Zapponin for this one," he said. "No need to re-etch engrams for these kinds of memories. All we want is to get her back to living a more productive life."

Marina eased the lady into the chair and fitted the headband to her small cranium. Dr. Blalock deftly injected part of the sedative into the lady's bony arm to ease her visible apprehension.

\* \* \* \*

The day finished with no failures or unexpected happenings, but a palpable air of gloom hung over the lab as Chelsea helped Danica file the day's case folders. "Sometimes, I really hate this work. It's so sad—I wish I could just limit my research to drunks and junkies who have fried their brains and just want to remember who they are and where they've been. The lady with the dead husband really got to me, not to mention the rape case. I really don't like reminding people about the horrors of their experiences. No—I think next quarter I'll stick to chemical abusers. Much more cheerful."

\* \* \* \*

William Henderson stepped into the lab, exuding confidence and positivity as he gazed directly and assuredly into Danica's eyes. "My dear, I'm not early, am I?"

"No—no you're...you're right on time. Please have a seat and remove your shirt...your new shirt. Dr. Waters will be in momentarily," Danica stammered in a suddenly thickened Spanish accent.

Chelsea stopped dead in her tracks as she fixed her gaze on Henderson seated at the console. A new liveliness and attentiveness sparked from him. Was that a smile? The change was astonishing. He had even bathed and shaved for the first time she could remember. "Will, you look great. How have you been doing?"

"Magnificently. I feel terrific. I remembered some more things. I remember being a kid, the friends I had, the places my family and I lived. I even remembered my first piece...the first time I was with a girl. I'm beginning to feel like a whole person."

"Will, you remembered all this on your own?" Chelsea gasped. None of what Henderson described had been on the last tape.

"Yeah, it just comes to me in a flood of revelation. It's wonderful," Henderson answered.

Puzzled as to Henderson's unassisted recall, Chelsea prompted the console, lost in a torrent of her own spinning thoughts. Marina injected the combination of Cerebrine and Zapponin as Chelsea settled back at her desk, intently watching Henderson ease out of the usual uncontrollable muscle tremor as scenes developed on the monitor.

Henderson must have spent a great deal of time on horseback judging from the many views of countryside sighted through the space between a horse's ears. Sounds of pounding hoofs and the low rhythmic grunting and huffing noises of horses in full gallop echoed into the lab.

Then, a great hall enveloped the entire screen as several seated people came into sight, all watching, all looking straight ahead, silent, motionless, mesmerized. A strong, resonant voice pierced the auditorium. It was unsettlingly familiar in quality, but not in force or conviction. The unseen voice described in meticulous detail parts of an epidemiological study—a study of neuroleptics and addiction. Chelsea's stomach lurched as she watched the screen, intrigued, and a little frightened.

As the drugs wore off, the screen danced with the usual discord characteristic of random thoughts. Chelsea flipped the monitor and audio output toggles, then removed the blinders and earmuffs from her patient.

Henderson said, "I was in college, wasn't I? I didn't know I went to college. I wonder what my major was. Could you make out what the professor was saying?"

Chelsea gathered her composure. "Barely. It was interesting, though. Do you remember what college it was? Do you know who the professor was?" she cautiously asked.

"No—not really. But I have a feeling I will real soon. Hey, maybe I can get a decent job if I have an education. I wonder what I'm good at? English, Accounting, Biology, Neur...." Henderson seemed to forget what he was going to say as he frowned, staring down at the floor.

"That'll do it for today, Will. Take it easy. You'll have plenty to discuss with your therapist when he sees this new recording. See you next week," Chelsea said.

"I want to come back tomorrow," Henderson demanded stubbornly.

"You have to see your therapist first, you know that. See him early tomorrow, and I'll squeeze you in for the afternoon. Is that alright?"

Chelsea's eye caught Danica's and Marina's stares as Henderson dressed and dashed out of the lab with his disk.

"What's wrong?" Danica asked.

"I don't know. I have this creepy feeling about Henderson. I wonder who he is," Chelsea said in an uneasy tone.

"Why? Because he went to college? What's so bad about that?" Danica inquired.

"Danica, you've been to college. When's the last time you were able to look into the audience and see all the other students staring back at you? During a speech, maybe? Were your fellow students ever riveted on your every word?" Chelsea asked.

"No, they always sat there just waiting for me to make a fool of myself," Danica said.

"Didn't you recognize the voice? And the vocabulary and subject matter? It was Henderson—*giving* a lecture on neurophysiology—not *taking* one!"

"Does he know?" Danica asked in a whisper.

"Not yet—but he will by tomorrow. Danica, page Beth. I hope you can both stay late tonight. I'm going to find out who this guy is." Chelsea stormed out of the lab and stepped onto a waiting elevator. Pushing the button for stratum three, she mentally composed what would become a blatant interrogation of Dr. Blalock.

"Dr. Blalock, this is Dr. Waters. Would you please grant me entry—it is of utmost importance," Chelsea said, pressing the intercom button near the sealed lab door.

"Come," Blalock grumbled.

Chelsea entered the huge microbiology lab. Every ghastly microbe known to man (and some unknown) was seething and multiplying in rows and rows of glass Petrie dishes and in bobbing, floating cylinders of test tubes suspended in anti-gravity chambers, defying anyone to gaze upon them, to jostle them, to unleash their unfathomable horror upon the world. This place welcomed a man such as Blalock; he belonged here, Chelsea thought.

"Dr. Waters, please state your business. I have dozens of samples to retest, and the lab must be cleared of all personnel but myself."

"I am concerned about one of my subjects. His last treatment revealed some lost memories which can only be interpreted as a previous occupation as neurophysiology professor. He had totally lost his memory of it—until today. I was hoping, since you knew almost everyone in the industry, that you could help us identify him," Chelsea said.

"What?" Dr. Blalock boomed. "What was his name?"

"William Henderson. Do you know him? He insists on coming back tomorrow for another treatment."

"No. Delay his treatment for at least a week. You're rushing him, it will only serve to confuse him," Blalock commanded.

"He's doing fine. Even his appearance has improved. Doctor, do you know who he might be?"

"Henderson? William Henderson? No. No—I don't know him. Please go now."

Chelsea was infuriated with Blalock's rudeness, but was not especially surprised that he would recommend putting the brakes on Henderson's recall treatments. He had been overly cautious ever since the accident in '84. Chelsea made her way back to stratum one where Beth and Danica impatiently waited for her in the hall.

"How goes it in the dragon's lair?" Beth chirped.

"Oh, the usual narrow-minded dogmatic stubbornness. He's worried Henderson may flip out if his past rushes in too quickly. He denies knowing Henderson or even hearing of him."

"So what do you need me for? Danica said it was urgent," Beth said.

"Henderson was a neurophysiology professor, but he doesn't remember it—yet. I want to know who he is, where he taught, where he worked. Is that possible?" Chelsea said.

"That's a tall order. It'll take the better part of the afternoon and evening," Beth said.

"Danica, I think we can handle this alone. You can go home."

"I'd rather stay, if you don't mind. Now, I'm curious."

Hours wore on as Beth typed in every version and spelling of William Henderson she could think of. Her efforts were fruitless. All database scans of personnel files for the entire west coast showed not even a glimmer of hope for matching Henderson up with a previous teaching position at any of the colleges or universities.

"Maybe William is his middle name," Danica said, freshly high on a cup of black coffee.

"Great!" Chelsea agreed.

Beth quickly typed in commands, recovering simultaneously all personnel files of the last learning institutions she had accessed. Watching screen after screen flip on then off, one screen of information remained. "My God. Look Chelsea! Robert William Henderson, professor of addictive neurophysiology, Northwest University, '77 through '83. He quit and became part of a classified research team at...."

"Where, where?" Chelsea insistently asked.

"It's locked. I can't go any further with this file. That's the way university security is most of the time."

Chelsea sank into a dispirited lump in her chair. She sat staring at the screen, trying to think of some lead, some clue that would reveal where Henderson had worked after he left the university.

"It's gotta be somewhere. I wonder if our files would...." Chelsea sat up sharply and touching Beth's arm to wake her from her daze, unintentionally ordered, "Check our personnel files for '83 through '84."

Obliging, Beth called up the institute's employee records. "Here it is! Chelsea, how did you know?"

"A devious hunch. It pays never to trust that bastard Blalock. Give me a print-out."

"I can't. Hard-copy print-out is disabled on this file. You have a good memory, start reading," Beth encouraged Chelsea.

Green phosphor letters stabbed at their eyes as Chelsea read aloud.

"That son-of-a-bitch Blalock! He worked with Henderson on the first team here! He lied to me."

"Look, he was fired in late '84 for boozing on the job. It seems his wife died just months before and he went off the deep end. How awful," Beth said.

"What did she die of, Beth?"

"Uh...let's see. Nope—I'll have to access another file. It sure would be easier if I knew *when* she died."

"Try early '84. She's in there—I know it," Chelsea said with certainty.

"March, '84. Here it is. Oh God, Chelsea, she's the one."

"The one what?" Chelsea leaned closer to the monitor screen, resting her chin on Beth's shoulder. "Oh God, I never knew the details. I never knew who it was or how it happened. So...it was Sally Henderson. She worked on the same team....No wonder Henderson's a drunkard."

"I don't exactly understand all the technical stuff here. What's it all mean?" Beth asked.

"It's one of the worst things that can happen in memory recovery. A feedback loop. It's the reason we have three people in the lab at all times during recall and recording. If the subject were to look at the screen or hear the sounds coming through the speakers at the same time he was internally experiencing them, he could get stuck in a feedback loop—possibly an endless one. Theoretically, the compounded thoughts gradually invade and overtake all other brain functions. No one really knows exactly what happens after that. Sally Henderson died when her husband unplugged the leads to the mainframe. No one knows why it killed her."

"How horrible. Henderson must feel responsible for his wife's death," Beth remarked.

"Yeah. Then that means not all of his memory loss is due to alcoholism. Blalock knows this. But, I can't figure why he didn't come right out and tell me. It would be nice if I knew what to expect when Henderson remembered his wife's death. We'd need Dr. Blalock in there to sedate him."

Beth shut down the computer terminal as Chelsea instructed Danica to finish cleaning up the lab and then lock up.

"Want to come over to my house for leftovers?" Chelsea asked Beth.

"Yeah, sure. You're leftovers can top anyone's first-runs."

\* \* \* \*

Beth opened the refrigerator door and stared in awe at the numerous neatly arranged plastic containers, all sporting a date and a letter prefix. "What's this? A damn filing system in here?"

"Yeah," Chelsea chuckled. "I have a food hierarchy in there—gotta eat what's most likely to spoil first, on down the line. It's the only way I could eliminate refrigerator horrors from my life. The A's should be eaten right away."

"The C's look more appetizing," Beth said.

"Lasagna—sounds terrific. I'll feed the A's to the neighbor's dog if they go bad."

Beth slipped two containers into the microwave, then ambled to the living room where Chelsea had just flopped on an over-stuffed sofa, sipping wine and gazing into the flickering flames in the fireplace.

"Tell me more about feedback loops, Chelsea. It's all so strange."

"Well, we really don't know a lot about the phenomenon. Except for Sally, no one's ever been in one long enough to find out what happens. The few patients who have been snapped out of one usually have a weird, blank expression on their faces. They don't remember going into it, or coming out. Of course, it's only a few seconds we're talking about here. Sally was trapped for over an hour before Henderson yanked the leads out in desperation." Chelsea reflected on the tragic death of Sally as she sipped her wine.

"Then, if someone gets stuck long enough, you can't get them out? What must that be like?" Beth asked.

"We think a feedback loop would be like a buzzing of convoluted thoughts, all folded into each other, forever repeating in layers. That's the abstract idea. Imagine you were on a multi-user chat forum where everyone you responded to was you, and everyone who responds is you—responding to you."

"Geez, it's like trying to ponder the size of the universe," Beth commented.

"Worse—the universe of the mind has no known boundaries. It is still the greatest mystery mankind has ever encountered.

"We just don't know enough about feedback loops to even dare to experiment with them. We don't know if they will eventually stop—if they are self-limiting. We don't know if they can kill. Sally died from being disconnected. I never even knew that until tonight. I read the media reports; there was no mention of how Sally died, just that she did—at our lab."

The conversation was interrupted by the shrill beeping of Chelsea's page unit. She rushed to the telephone and dialed the institute.

"This is Dr. Waters responding to page," she said.

"Dr. Waters, Dr. Blalock is ordering your presence at the institute immediately. Please enter through the service door," a voice said. A harsh honking sound screamed over the phone lines from the background. The line went silent.

Chelsea stood petrified, staring into the flames, still holding the phone at shoulder level.

"Chelsea, are you alright?"

"Red alert. There's a Goddamned red alert at the lab. God, it's got to be bad news at this hour, " Chelsea said glancing at her watch. " Blalock's probably accidentally let some of his recombinant DNA creatures loose. Last time this happened, I was in the hospital for a month with some exotic infection. He's done it again. Dammit!

"Stay here, Beth. I'll fill you in later."

"No way, I'm going with you. Where's your keys? I'm driving," Beth said assuredly.

"Beth, you can be such an ass—and such a great friend."

\* \* \* \*

The front entrance to the institute was as dark and impenetrable as if it had been closed permanently. Chelsea could hear the faint whine of the indoor red alert siren as Beth steered the car around to the back of the building, parking haphazardly near the service entrance.

Chelsea forced the four successive keys into their appropriate locks, and rushed with Beth through the blood-red lighted hallway to the elevator. Before she could summon it, the door snapped open and Dr. Blalock stepped off, belly first.

"Dr. Blalock! You shouldn't be off stratum three—you'll contaminate the whole building!" Chelsea exclaimed. "How...how did you get down to this level—the elevators don't work if there's a breach...."

"The emergency is on *this* floor, Dr. Waters," Blalock said.

Chelsea was frozen in disbelief, unable to articulate words that would make sense.

Beth stepped beside Chelsea. "What's the problem—where's the problem?"

"Someone is holding Miss Ortega at gunpoint in the Neural Lab. He threatened to kill her if he's not connected to the computer right away," Blalock said bluntly.

"My God, she's still here? Who's in there with her? How long...." Chelsea's voice faded into a gagged realization of horror.

"This has been going on since ten-thirty. Ortega had some filing to do, eh? She's not lucky tonight," Blalock said.

Chelsea's patience was eroding. "Who's holding her, damn you?"

Blalock hesitated in his usual sadistic manner. "Why, your star patient—William Henderson. The police will be here soon."

A surge of almost uncontrollable anger swept through Chelsea's body as she contemplated murdering Blalock where he stood. "Shut up, you old fart! You lied to me about knowing Henderson. I know, you bastard. I know you worked with him!"

"It's not important—none of your business," Blalock retorted.

"The hell it's not! Henderson's past is of utmost importance when we're drudging up suppressed memories! You know that, asshole!"

Without saying another word, Blalock turned and stomped down the hallway to the service door where two policemen had just let themselves in. Blalock led them up the hall, loudly explaining the situation to them.

"Sergeant Perry, this is Dr. Chelsea Waters. The man holding the woman hostage is her patient."

"Dr. Chelsea, what can you tell me about the patient?" the Sergeant asked.

"It's Dr. Waters...dammit I just got here. Blalock, will you reset the alarm system? I can't even hear myself think."

Beth took her cue and stepped in beside Chelsea. "I'm Beth Johnston. I'm with the institute. What would you like to know?"

"What's he being treated for? Is he on drugs, prescribed or otherwise? What are his demands and what has he threatened to do if they aren't met?" Sergeant Perry was precise in his questioning.

"He's being treated for alcoholic brain syndrome. Dr. Blalock tells us he is demanding to be reconnected to the computer, or he will kill our lab assistant. That's all we know," Beth coolly explained.

"Has anyone talked to him recently—tried to talk him out?

Sergeant Perry asked.

"No, Blalock deflected us from that," Chelsea snapped.

"Can these treatments be addictive at all?" Sergeant Perry asked.

"No—not at all. He is so happy with his newly discovered past, he's been very eager for additional treatments. It's a fairy normal reaction in these people. I wouldn't call it addictive—just childishly impatient," Chelsea explained.

"Can you get in there and talk to him? Get him to back off. Find out why he can't wait for his treatment. There's got to be a reason," Sergeant Perry suggested.

Chelsea approached the lab door and looked through the small glass window. Henderson sat on Chelsea's desk, loosely holding a pistol, minimally threatening Danica with it as she sat to his right at her desk. Danica seemed more tired than anything else.

Henderson looked up. An expression of recognition washed over his worried face.

Chelsea knocked, then slowly open the door to the lab, allowing her empty hands to precede her. "It's Chelsea, Will. Talk to me. Tell me why you can't wait until tomorrow."

"I have a wife. I'm married. Where is she? I remembered her, I saw her in my thoughts—no, I couldn't really *see* her—I *felt* her. I can't remember what she looks like...her name...."

A wife, Will?" Chelsea asked stupidly. "You're listed as single in your medical file. I don't understand, Will. Why do you think you have a wife?"

"Because I do! The file's wrong—you're wrong! Hook me up—now!" Henderson waved the pistol in Danica's direction.

Chelsea flinched as she saw Danica's internal terror well forth in a gasp and whimper. "Everything's going to be alright, Will. We'll hook you up tomorrow, as I promised. Let Danica go—she's only a lab assistant. She can't help you."

"I want my wife back! I want to remember her—I have to find her!" Grasping the pistol with both hands and pointing it at Danica, he squeezed off a shot, planting a bullet in the wall just above her head. Danica's eyes rolled back as she slumped into a cold faint on the floor at the corner of her desk. "I'll kill her! I swear I'll kill her if you don't hook me up!" Henderson raved.

Chelsea could hardly breathe. A suffocating grip disabled her airways as she fought to exhale. A pounding pulse jerked through her frightened veins. She now realized she had no choice but to connect Henderson to the computer.

Moving cautiously, she announced her intention to leave the lab to consult with Blalock and Beth. Henderson motioned a concession and allowed Chelsea to leave.

"Sergeant—he's adamant. He remembers a wife and wants to complete the engram re-etching," Chelsea panted.

Blalock moved his bulk forward, intruding upon the private circle of confidants. "A wife? That can't be!" he blurted.

Chelsea felt a tremendous surge of adrenalin gush into her every cell. She was the most angry she had been in years. "Why not, Blalock? What else are you not telling me?"

"We erased those memories. We erased them when he was fired from here. He doesn't know what happened with his wife—that he even had a wife. He doesn't remember he worked for us. This can't be."

Chelsea went silent for several seconds, then barked, "Erased? You can't *erase* memories—all you can do is *suppress* them! You incompetent boob! I'm filing a full report on this activity in the morning. Get fitted for a Chef's hat, Fritz. You're outta here!"

Chelsea stormed off down the hall, busting into the lab, forgetting the danger waiting for her there. Henderson turned abruptly, removing his aim from Danica and directing it onto Chelsea. "Dammit, Will! Put that thing away! I'm gonna hook you up—just knock off the Jesse James act!"

Henderson quaked as he held the gun pointing straight at Chelsea's head. "No—you're lying. Who's out there waiting for me? What's going on?"

"The police, Will. They sent me in here to talk to you—but they won't come in as long as I'm in here."

"Henderson raised his arms, grasping the pistol with both hands. "And to make sure they won't...."

Chelsea found herself staring down the smoky barrel of an almost fully loaded revolver.

Five bullets waited to rip through her brain on their way to the glass in the door behind her. Chelsea was mortified and stood frozen as images of a bloody death careened through her mind. Her pounding heart slammed blood against her artery walls in great pulsating gushes that threatened to explode her head. Tears began to run silently down her cheeks as she struggled to remove her gaze from the gun and make eye contact with Henderson. "Will," Chelsea said in a disguised tremble, "if you kill me, you'll never see your wife again—you'll never find her."

"You know where she is?"

"No—but you do. It's all locked up in your mind—the way she

looks, her name, everything about her. You know where you can find her. Let me hook you up, Will."

Henderson lowered the gun, backed away and positioned himself in the chair near the console. "Do it now. I want it now."

Danica was just regaining consciousness as Chelsea slowly moved towards her desk to retrieve the syringe and the two vials Danica had been forced to get under the duress of Henderson's pistol.

Chelsea spoke precisely and calmly. "Danica, do you feel well enough to help me hook up Will to the computer? Will needs this."

Henderson had already removed his shirt before Danica was up off the floor. He watched her intently, suspiciously, as she seated the headband around his skull. He hardly flinched when Chelsea slid the needle into his carotid artery.

Just as Danica eased the blinders over Henderson's eyes, he forcefully grabbed her wrist. "No blinders!" he snapped.

"O.K., but no looking at the screen. Promise?" Chelsea said with a contrived sweet, understanding smile. Henderson nodded. Checking the earmuffs for a secure fit, Chelsea flipped toggle switches on the console, and settled back at her desk.

Images quickly formed on the screen, more quickly than usual. Voices rang out into the lab. Henderson sat stiffly, holding the pistol in a guarded grip, ready to fire another shot at the first indication of betrayal from Danica. Chelsea stood at his side, remaining within his range of vision.

The scenes flowed onto the giant screen; sweet lovers' conversation saturated the coldness of the lab. Henderson watched Danica's frightened breathing as he held her captive in the pistol's aim.

Henderson closed his eyes as images of Sally's creamy-complexioned face glowed in his mind and formed on the screen behind him. An almost imperceptible trail of tears trickled down his smiling face.

Suddenly, in a rush of distrust, Henderson flashed open his eyes, only to catch Danica making her way to the lab door. He raised the pistol and impulsively pulled the trigger, burying a burning bullet in her right shoulder. Danica cursed in Spanish, smashing against the door, holding the fresh wound with her left hand. Behind her, police officers peered in, changing places, pushing each other away from the porthole, then pushing back into view. Beth's face appeared then disappeared as the police officers crowded in around the glass to look inside the lab, rattling the locked door in vain.

In an instantaneous, furious and insane spasm of hatred, Chelsea spun Henderson's chair around to face the screen. Henderson's astonished face became patterned with the mosaic of Sally's naked body flickering on the screen. He sat absolutely motionless, mouth hanging open and staring expressionless at his own swirling, overlaid thoughts. Chelsea removed the earmuffs and cranked up the audio output, then rushed to help Danica out of the lab.

"My God, I heard a shot, but I couldn't see anything," Beth anxiously said.

"Danica's been hit. It's not serious. Beth, can you get her to the hospital?"

"What's Henderson doing? We're going in!" Sergeant Perry insisted.

"No. Leave him be. There's no cause for alarm—he won't be bothering anyone anymore," Chelsea said.

"Is he dead?" Sergeant Perry asked.

"No—not yet. Just...don't go in there."

"Lady, if he's sick or injured, we gotta call an ambulance. If not, we gotta take him in. He's broken into a secured research facility and shot a hostage!"

"He's already been exiled to the worst prison conceivable—he's stuck in a feedback loop," Chelsea smugly explained.

"A what?"

Sergeant Perry obviously would have to have everything explained to him. This was something Chelsea did not particularly look forward to at this moment. "Would someone mind getting us some coffee? This is going to take a while."

Chelsea watched Sergeant Perry's face contort in disbelief as she detailed what little she could tell him about Henderson's predicament.

The Sergeant eased up to the glass in the door and peered into the lab, squinting to discern the patterns on the monitor before Henderson's transfixed gaze. "It looks like a kaleidoscope...like electricity gone crazy in there."

"A single thought, added to itself and squared a million times," Chelsea softly remarked. She got up from the bench in the hall and opened the door to the lab to listen. A sound like a huge crowd screaming gushed out of the speakers, ensnaring Henderson in an indescribable cacophony of nonsense.

"What happens next?" asked the Sergeant.

"We wait. If we disconnect him, he dies. If we don't...I have no idea what will happen. I'm planning to stay awake for it, whatever it turns out to be."

\* \* \* \*

Lying on the hall bench with a wet cloth draped across her forehead, Chelsea barely caught a glimpse of Beth stumbling into the foyer from the main entrance.

It was light out, but amazingly there were no reporters—no one had caught wind of the historical disaster unfolding in the Neural Tracing Lab. Those present were either exhausted, as Chelsea, or occupied as the young officer who retched and vomited into the hall drinking fountain. Blalock was nowhere to be seen.

"Jesus, what's going on here?" Beth quizzed.

"Chelsea strained into an upright position as she groped for Beth's arm to help her up. "The cops aren't taking this too well, and I'm...I'm mostly without explanation," Chelsea groggily answered.

"What? What can't you explain?"

"What's happened to Henderson—it's incredible. It's absolutely ungodly."

"Beth rushed to the window glass in the lab door, cupping her hands around her face, trying to see in the subdued lighting, anxiously jerking at the unyielding door handle.

"No Beth! You can't go in there!" Chelsea shrieked as she clutched the wet cloth to her head.

"Girl, you're white as a ghost. What's going on in there? And why are the lights out?"

"Oh Beth—it's horrible. I never would have predicted...if this gets out, we're—I'm—ruined," Chelsea said as she swayed sitting on the bench.

A mechanical clang tore through the emptiness of the foyer. Two reporters with their troop of cameras had entered. One burly reporter burst into the hall, armed with a microphone, camera technicians trailing. "Leonard Glaski, KGA-TV. We have received an anonymous call that there is a patient holding a lab assistant hostage in your lab, demanding to be connected to the computer. Can you give us any details?"

Chelsea collapsed on the bench, shifting the cloth down over her eyes. *Not again. This can't be happening again. Blalock, you dog-drool. You called this in to save your own fat ass. You know just where to hit me—you bastard,* Chelsea mentally ranted. Peeking from beneath a corner of the cloth, she saw Beth defiantly stomp up to the reporter, ordering, "The institute will not be open to the public for another two hours. Please leave. You are trespassing. We have two police officers to escort you out."

"Ma'am, what are the police doing here? Do you usually have officers here at the institute? What's happening?" the reporter demanded. Beth motioned to Sergeant Perry and the queasy-green young rookie, who immediately sprinted into action to deflect the reporters and their crew. She knelt to Chelsea, shaking her shoulders. "Tell me what the hell's going on, Chelsea. What's in the lab? Let me in." Impulsively, Beth reached down and snatched the keys from Chelsea's waist belt. She rammed a key into the lab door lock, and slowly creaked the door open, reaching inside to feel for the light switch. The banks of fluorescent tubes flashed on, illuminating the unspeakable drama taking place in front of the giant sizzling monitor.

Chelsea lurched up and pushed her way into the lab past Beth, and reeled around to face her, still clutching the cloth to her beating temple vessels. "Dammit, Beth!"

"My God!" Beth half gasped, half whimpered. "Is...is *that* him?"

"What's left of him. Let's get out of here, Beth." Chelsea tugged at Beth's arm, failing to budge her. Beth was solidly anchored to the floor, her gaze cemented to the grisly spectacle before them.

Henderson's lobed brain protruded from a freshly cracked fissure in the top of his skull as rhythmic spurts of arterial blood bespeckled the console and rained on the floor around him. It reminded Chelsea of some kind of nightmarish lawn sprinkler, spraying his life frivolously all about him. The flesh on the near side of his face quivered as hideous gobs of vileness gurgled from his ears, boiling over onto his rigid shoulders as it foamed, trickled, plopped to the floor.

The screen buzzed furiously; the roar of a crowd of a single voice echoed throughout the lab. Chelsea left Beth and apprehensively approached the voluminous foulness of Henderson's fate. She dared to step beside his fizzing mass to catch a glimpse of his face. His eyes had completely exploded from their orbits, dangling like cooked okra on his quivering cheeks. Pus-like ooze seeped from the empty sockets, soaking his chest hair in sticky, matted swirls.

Then, the screen abruptly blinked off; the crowd of voices became mute. The lab was still and silent as Chelsea stared in horrified curiosity at the remains of Henderson's last morbid seconds of life. She felt a wave of relieved nausea sweep over her as she went back towards Beth, who still stood entranced near the door. "Now we know what happens when someone gets left in a feedback loop," Chelsea said weakly.

Beth staggered into the hall as Chelsea pushed her through the door from behind.

"God, Chelsea. What did happen? Why didn't he just go catatonic and die—neatly, cleanly, dignified?"

"His brain was filled—the same thought, re-etched over and over again. It all had to go somewhere. There just wasn't enough room...so much for the infinite universe of the mind."

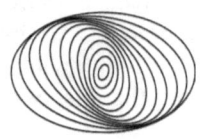

# FINAL THOUGHTS

As my life literally flashes before my eyes, I consider how it is that I've been put in this most depressing of situations. The bipedal monsters, their forelegs so agile and flexible, have brought us here, crowded together in our stench and misery, this unfamiliar place our last habitat.

We begin to move in a single direction, orbiting an unseen center, our fear-shit oozing between our toes. The movement helps us deal with our impending deaths, the deaths of our friends and relatives. We, the living, must behave similarly to atomic particles, wherein electrons must maintain their own territorial energy levels so they don't collapse into each other. But unlike atomic particles, our mass cannot increase the gravitational effect on spacetime, curving it even more. We are too confined. If we could move faster we might even be able to condense space while dilating our experience in time. But this is prevented us by our mere confinement.

But then, all particles exist as probability waves, not as "real" particles—much in contrast with the macro world of our five physical senses. I am reminded all too frequently by the buffeting of living bodies, that I am of that world.

The air is saturated with the blood of those who have died before us. Death cries and moans portend our fate.

I'd like to be next to my brother, feel his warmth against my skin before it's snuffed out forever. But he is far from me, hundreds of bodies away across the knot of life that we comprise.

I remember especially his eyes. He would have been an irresistible mate to some lucky female—had the bipeds not castrated him. They had castrated all us males, to make us less aggressive, make us docile, lethargic, and fat. It isn't a natural thing.

"Brother, did any of us predict we would not live out our lives in peace?" I thought-voice to him. "Did any of us see this coming?"

"Do not lament, dear brother. Time is spherical. Past, present, and future coexist. We are already dead; we have not been born. It is what it is."

"You do not grieve the experience? Fear the pain?"

"In my last minutes, I find solace in the non-locality of the universe. Reality is all one point. Everything is connected to everything else," he says.

Someone slammed into me, loosing his footing in the slime of our own feces. I collect my thoughts. "How is this a comfort, dear brother? How does this help you—help me—in dealing with our impending termination? How does believing it has been so since The First Spark, help? How does it help to know that all energy knots with previous contact shall forever be correlated?"

"These creatures who imprison and murder us, they do not understand. They—though arrogant enough to be technologically superior—are ignorant and incapable of comprehending their connectedness. They do not understand that we are not simply a collection of unrelated parts, but the parts are complete representations of the whole. When they kill representations of their universe, they kill themselves. They kill us without apology, without remorse, with no sense of loss. Their hunger is their justification. It is not important that they understand. It is only important that we do."

His logic does not make me feel any better. The time is near—I smell it.

"Every exit is an entrance to someplace else," he says as he gravitates towards his end. "We don't live or die in the first and only oscillation we have or ever will experience. We are part of the oscillation. See you next oscillation, dear brother."

The bipeds push him through a chute and press a long pole to the flat part of his head. A buzz splits the air. My brother stiffens, eyes staring into eternity.

The bipeds rip a hook through his hind leg, just above the hock. My brother never makes a sound, Universe bless him.

See you next oscillation, brother.

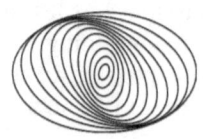

# FUNERARIUM

"And how long has this been going on?"

"About four years now—off and on. I never really know when it's going to happen. Sometimes I go two or three months—and nothing. Other times it happens every night, or even in the morning.

"It's the same every time. First, it's dark. Then I see it—just for a few seconds. Then, it's all black again. It's exactly the same every time, like it's been taped or something. There's no variation—ever."

Beata's hands were sweaty and trembled almost imperceptibly. Her pulse throbbed throughout her body. Even her hair pulsed, and she imagined it must be visible to anyone watching her. She fought to maintain control of her surging emotions.

"Can you describe it to me, in detail?" The psychiatrist was a gentle Asian man, quiet and relaxed in manner, but offering very little feedback.

"Yeah, I could even draw you a picture of it."

"Then, would you do that for me? Now?"

Dr. Sherman handed Beata his clipboard and pen.

Beata sketched out a lawn, adding distant trees, then she began the outline of the headstone, carefully aligning the letters and shading them to make them appear etched. She finished with the lady's bare lower legs, black high heels, and the bottom of the black knee-length dress.

Showing minor pride in her artistic talents, Beata returned the clipboard to Dr. Sherman. "That's it. Nothing more, nothing less."

Dr. Sherman studied the rendering in silence, betraying his detached calmness with the rapidly jerking foot of his crossed leg. "Why did you misspell your name?" he asked.

"That's the way it always looks. Very few people could ever spell it right, I'm not surprised it's misspelled." Beata answered uncaring and resigned.

"And it's your maiden name. Have you ever been married, Beata? Would you like to be some day?"

"No on both counts. Life is full of limitations. Why would I want to add yet another?"

"Is this all you ever see, just the headstone and up to the lady's hem?" The doctor seemed very interested now as he leaned forward in his chair, focusing intently on every word Beata uttered.

"Yep...like a cropped photo. I don't even know who that lady is."

"That was going to be my next question." He paused, tipped his gold wire-framed glasses with his left hand, recrossed his legs to the other side, and said, "How do you feel about this dream...do you believe it's a prediction?"

Beata hesitated, avoiding eye contact while fingering the folds and brushing the nap of her green corduroy dress. "I don't know. I guess that's why I'm here. Is this normal? What happens to people who have recurring dreams like this? Do the dreams ever go away...do they come true?"

"It's not an altogether uncommon occurrence. Usually it's due to stress. Are you dealing with your illness in a constructive way, Beata? Tell me about an average day." His condescending and evasive demeanor infuriated Beata.

"Horseshit, Doc. Lupus is a mother, it's extremely painful, it's energy-robbing, and it sometimes kills. We both know that. Answer my questions. Do the dreams go away on their own or come true or... what? What am I going to do?"

Remaining unaffected by her obvious irritation, Dr. Sherman said, "Most of the time they do go away spontaneously—if whatever is stressing the person is relieved. As for coming true, well..." He attempted to conceal a smile as he continued. "Many people insist on finding meaning in unrelated events. Coincidence is a powerful drug. Do you really believe that you will die on September ninth, nineteen ninety-two?"

"Jesus, you're such a damn minimalist. If the stress is relieved—which in my case is constant pain—then I must be dead! Sure as shit, the dreams will go away then. Thanks, Einstein." Beata completely lost control and gushed forth with the suppressed fear and grief welling up over the last hour. She again felt the absolute hopelessness, the control the dream had over her. The doctor could be of no help, she reasoned. He couldn't possibly understand what it was like to see your own grave visited time after time for four years—by the same unknown lady—what it was like to see your name misspelled for the last time, knowing you will die on September 9TH, 1992. There was so little time left; she suddenly resented wasting it in a shrink's office, and pushed her aching body up from the chair.

"Beata, would you consider undergoing hypnosis for this problem, say, next session? It will help you deal with your agitation, and perhaps, if you respond well, together we can purge those dreams once and for all." Dr. Sherman seemed more sincere and genuinely concerned than he had been in the past.

"Well, isn't that something. It would be a pleasant change—to have you actually *doing* something, instead of just sitting there nodding your head in agreement like a foreigner that doesn't understand English—no offense. Yeah, I'm game. See you next week with my tape recorder." Beata limped out of the office, wiping away the makeup that she felt caking up under her eyes.

\* \* \* \* \*

It was a cool, misty California fall morning. There was no breeze and the tree branches hung in an undisturbed droop, mourning the dead in their characteristic eucalyptus sorrow. The grass had been freshly mowed.

She walked to the dull gray headstone, turning gracefully on her toes to avoid hooking the long spike heels in the matted lawn. Beyond the full calves of her nyloned legs, just beneath the black hem of her skirt, the letters on the granite stared out coldly:

BEATA FERGUSON
Born April 28, 1955 — Died Sept. 9, 1992
"I TOLD YOU SO."

Beata woke in a deep, dripping sob. She stiffly rolled over and groped for a tissue to blow her stuffed-up nose. The fifth night in a row, she lamented. Will it never stop...will it goddamn never stop? Beata continued to cry. She turned on the lamp and compulsively, desperately began a detailed, meticulous charcoal and colored pencil drawing of her haunting. Maybe if she captured it on paper as carefully as possible, as precisely as a photograph, she could remove it from her thoughts, her dreams, her very life. If she could imprison it on paper and let her mind rest....

\* \* \* \* \*

"I'm going to count to three. You will be in a fully relaxed and receptive state. You will hear only my voice as you allow me to guide you to inner peace and harmony." Dr. Sherman spoke in a slow, deliberate and metered monotone.

"The recurring dream you have been having is being misinterpreted. What you think is a headstone is really a cornerstone for a new building being erected. The lettering states the name of the contractor, the starting date and the ending date for the construction project. It has nothing to do with death, but signals the beginning and perfection of something that will stand and be useful and admired for many years to come."

As the weeks passed, Dr. Sherman gradually convinced Beata that she didn't see what she saw in her dream. Although the dream was occurring more often, sometimes even several times nightly, it had no emotional impact, no meaning for Beata.

The blistering, suffocating heat of August made for a last miserable session. Beata had considered cancelling it, but succumbed to the persuasive urgings of Dr. Sherman. Though the dream no longer bothered her, Dr. Sherman planned one last session to evict the dream from her mind forever. He instructed her to vanish the dream completely, willing it gone and finished.

"Do you remember anything about the dream? Anything at all?" he asked cautiously.

Beata stared into space, fully conscious, but visibly stunned. "My God...no—I don't. Nothing! That's amazing! For the first time in three months, you've actually earned your pay. I'm impressed, Dr. Sherman. I'm free of it. I really believe I am free of it!" The sting of mascara-tainted tears filled her eyes as she smiled a relieved, liberated smile.

She was finally emancipated from the horrifying grip of the dream. It no longer owned her—not her thoughts, not her artwork, not her sleep. She got up, forgetting to even say good-bye or thank you, and left the office in a slow, stupefied daze.

\* \* \* \* \*

"Hello, may I speak with Dr. Sherman?" Beata asked as she twirled the telephone cord around her fingers and wrist.

"Dr. Sherman is with a patient. Are you a patient of his?" the receptionist politely inquired.

"Yes, this is Beata Furgesun. It's important."

Two minutes passed and Dr. Sherman came on the line. "Yes, Beata, how are you feeling? I haven't seen you in a while. Is everything all right?"

"Did I have an appointment today? It seems to me that I had an appointment with you...or something important...." Beata's voice faded.

"You could have asked the receptionist if you were scheduled. Is something bothering you Beata? If you need to come in, I can squeeze you in."

"No...it's just I have this strange, gnawing feeling I was supposed to be somewhere today. Are you sure you didn't have me scheduled for September ninth?"

Dr. Sherman's abrupt silence caused a sickening apprehension in her. She became confused, anxious, angry. "What's wrong, Doc?" she demanded. "Did I say something I shouldn't have?"

"Have you been sleeping well, Beata?"

"Yeah, sure. Like a corpse. What's that got to do with anything?"

"Beata...at the risk of losing everything we've worked for over these last weeks...I have to tell you, I guess."

The psychiatrist paused for what seemed like minutes. Beata listened to the silence build up over the phone lines; it beat at her eardrums. Fear strangled her words. She wanted to ask the next question, but couldn't.

"Beata, today's the day you were convinced you were going to die. It's a fantasy, Beata. No connection to reality. The dream is gone. It no longer exists. You're going to be OK, trust me. Can you come in today around four o'clock? We can reinforce your treatment—sort of like a booster shot."

"No! I'm not leaving the house. Shit—I knew something was wrong! How can you expect me to even get in a car? Or the elevator? You must be nuts!"

"Beata, will you call me tonight at my home, at midnight? You have to be convinced that nothing is going to happen to you. Everything's going to be all right. Stay home if you like, but promise you'll call me. Will you?"

"OK, OK. I have a feeling I'll be on the phone a lot today and tonight. What's one more call?"

\* \* \* \* \*

"Hello?" a feminine voice said.

"Yes, this is Beata Furgesun. Dr. Sherman asked me to call him. I'm a patient."

"Yes, one moment, Beata. He's expecting your call."

"Hello, Beata. It's eleven fifty-seven. How are you feeling?" The psychiatrist's voice was positive and soothing.

"Well, nothing bad has happened to me yet. Not even a close call. I still feel strange, though. There's three minutes left you know," she said defiantly.

"Then talk to me, Beata. Tell me what you did today, who you talked to. Before you know it, it'll be September tenth, and you can kiss your superstition good-bye once and for all," Dr. Sherman patiently reassured her.

Beata talked in jerky, nervous staccato as she continuously glanced at the clock on her nightstand. The red numbers screamed at her, seared into her eyeballs through the dim lighting of her bedroom. The digital characters seemed to form in a leisurely, miserable ooze, deliberately taunting her, slowly amplifying her tension as they advanced the time in their horrid satanic scarlet display.

"Beata, look—it's twelve ten. September tenth! You're OK. I told you, Beata. I told you. Beata?" Dr. Sherman waited for a response; there was none. "Beata...Beata? Answer me, Beata!"

Beata lay still on her bed, her eyes wide open and fixed on a point on the ceiling, clutching the phone receiver to her chest as Dr. Sherman's pleas danced off her sternum from the receiver speaker.

"Beata! Answer me! Is this some kind of joke?" Dr. Sherman's emotions spilled out in full force now. He was as out of control as any of his patients could be.

"I'm sorry. I'm OK, I'm OK," Beata said as she moved the receiver to her ear. "I'm sorry. I was just in some kind of shock. It's so unreal. Thank you, Dr. Sherman. You were right. I'll see you tomorrow. I'll definitely see you tomorrow."

* * * * *

The air was thick with a crystal, cool, bluish fog. The mist collected and dripped from the pendulous tree leaves, soaking the newly cut grass beneath the forever solemn eucalyptus. There was a musty scent of fresh, newly turned earth in the thick, wet, motionless air.

She stepped carefully up to the dreary granite headstone, turning on the ball of her feet to keep her shoe heels from catching in the sod. "It was a very small turn-out, wouldn't you say?" Mrs. Sherman remarked to her husband.

"Yes. Small. I still can't believe it. The autopsy said she died of natural causes. That's just coroner jargon for 'we don't know.' My God, she was only thirty-seven."

"What a shame they misspelled her last name. And such a sloppy job on the engraving...you can barely make out the '1' before the '9' on the date of death," Mrs. Sherman said.

"Yeah. Neither could she."

# AWWW...BABY GATORS!

We were pretty ripped by the time we got back to the boat. Robby tripped over his feet as we waded back into the water. I laughed, drunkenly, half expecting him to dive face-first into the murky Lake Apopka water. Alcohol and water don't mix, but I laughed anyway. He could drown—I'd probably still laugh. Robby thrashed around a bit, but managed to right himself in the dark, groping for the little sliver of boat he could see shining in the lights of the cantina behind him, pulling himself over and into the boat with the grace of a drugged walrus.

This was our summer Friday night ritual—cash our paychecks, spend a half-hour priming and swearing at the motor on our beat up outboard, and chug on down the lake in the dark to our shoreline sanctuary. The nights were suffocating and sticky, the beer cold, the music loud, and the girls few. It was our little slice of Heaven in Florida's backwoods hell.

"Hey, Alex. Look," Robby half-whispered. "A baby gator."

"Where?" I said dumbly, stumbling into the boat, not even looking to where Robby pointed somewhere in the dark.

"Over there," he said. "Just beyond that knot of grass."

I strained to see in the dark, squinted to make the two images merge into one. "Oh yeah, I see it!" It glistened like a wet slug on the shore. Robby punched me for raising my voice. "I see another one... over there," whispering now, pointing down shore.

"And there's *another* one...*oh shit,*" Robby said.

"What's wrong? Oh shit, what?"

"Where there's babies, there's momma. We better get outta here," Robby said.

No sooner had Robby grabbed for the anchor—a cinder block on the end of a polyethylene rope—than we heard a loud splash at the bow. Another splash, and another. I scrambled to start the motor—one rip, then two. It started! We lunged into the dark, turning sharply, jaws snapping at the wake behind us.

The boat labored up shore. Were we moving? Jaws still snapped behind us, getting closer, closer. We should be outrunning momma gator. The motor moaned, the boat slowed and choked. Robby yanked on the rope to no avail. "Aw man, it weighs a ton! Must've dragged big wads of crap from the bottom of the lake. Alex, get the knife!"

Before I could remember where I put it, the boat suddenly stopped, spilling us to our knees. With a final grinding gasp, the motor quit altogether. Snapping jaws drew closer, butted against the stern of the boat with a sloshy thud. The alligator swam slowly from side to side at the stern, tail making thick ripples in the water.

"This rope ain't budgin' one inch," Robby panted, tugging on the slippery line.

I tried to start the motor. I couldn't even pull the cord—it was stuck. "The anchor line's wrapped around the propeller, I just know it" I mumbled.

"It's *what*? Naw, don't say that! We're stuck in the middle of this lake with a gator on our asses—don't say that!"

Sighing, I looked down shore. The lights from the cantina pierced tiny pinholes in the steamy night air. We'd moved maybe fifty feet. Through the bushes just up shore, music played, a fire blazed. I heard water lapping against the shore, punctuated by the intestinal growl of Harley engines. Momma gator turned and swam, turned and swam at the stern of our crippled outboard. An impending hangover was fighting for attention in the recesses of my skull.

I stared at Robby, now sitting in the boat with his head in his hands. "You know, of course, that *someone* has to get out and cut the fucking rope," I said. I don't know why I wanted it to sound so plausible. It wasn't. Momma gator made sure of that.

Robby looked up, expressionless. "First one to finish that bottle of Tequila in the tackle box gets nominated." He burst out laughing. I couldn't help it, as much as I tried, I held my throbbing head and laughed too—painfully, dryly, until I almost puked.

A bloodshot ribbon of dawn oozed up over the horizon. My shoulder hurt from sleeping on the tackle box all night. Robby was curled up in a little greasy ball, hugging a half-empty tequila bottle, a grin warping his face.

"Hey," I said, kicking Robby's left foot. "Momma gator's gone. We need to cut that rope loose and get outta here." My shoulder was loosening up.

Robby groaned and shielded his eyes as a dagger of sunlight skewered his pupils. He tossed the bottle aside and sat up. "What's this 'we' crap?"

"Com'on! I need to keep a lookout in case momma gator comes back. And to start the boat."

Robby scowled. "Wait a minute. There's something missing. I think you left out the part where you get my ass back in the boat. *Then* you start the motor. Christ, Alex. Some friend."

"Alright. Alright. Go down there and cut the rope off the prop, will you?"

Without looking up, Robby threw his body over the edge of the boat into the brown water; it only came to his neck. I handed him the Bowie knife from the tackle box. "You beat on the bottom of the boat if you see momma gator anywhere, OK?" Without waiting for my answer, his head disappeared under the water.

About twelve seconds later I stamped my feet furiously on the bottom of the boat. A jet of tan water shot up near the stern, followed by a water-logged gasp, limbs flailing in the air, Robby's body spilling into the boat. I nearly barfed I laughed so hard. "Shit, Robby," I howled, "I never seen you move so fast in my life!"

Robby grinned and snapped up the bottle of tequila, unscrewing the cap and knocking back a giant gulp. "Asshole," he wheezed. In one seamless motion, he wiped his mouth, jumped back in the water and went under with the knife. Thirty seconds later he came up, took a big breath, and went back under. The fourth time he came up, he took a big breath, said "Goddammit" and dove back under again. Seven dives later, he pulled himself back into the boat.

"Rope's too hard. It's wrapped around the prop real good. Knife won't cut through."

If Robby couldn't cut it, I sure as hell couldn't. Though I would never admit it to him, he was stronger than I was. What we needed was some serious muscle...or a bigger knife. About then I looked up and saw a motorcycle emerge from the bushes on shore. The big bearded man dismounted and waddled to the lake's edge, water lapping his boots as a rainbow streamed from his groin in the morning sun.

"Hey!" I yelled. "Hey, can you help us?"

Robby grabbed my arm. "What, are you nuts?"

The big man seemed to be concentrating on his business as I kept yelling, trying to loosen Robby's grip. Finally, he zipped his fly and looked up and stared for a few seconds.

"Hey! We're dead in the water here! Can you give us a hand?" I hollered.

The man turned and walked back to his bike, kicked it to life and drove back through the bushes.

"I coulda told you he wouldn't help us. I'm surprised he didn't shoot you, screamin' at him in the middle of a whiz like that." Robby was stronger than me, but he was a wuss sometimes.

Before I could answer, a hoard of leather, denim, and T-shirts waded into the water and loomed towards us. It was our worst nightmare—even worse than being marooned on a lake at night in a boat with an anchor line wrapped around the prop while a gator snaps at your stern. The Hell's Angels were going to beat us, rape us, take our boat and drink the rest of our tequila. We were going to die a humiliating death. Somehow being gator chow would have been more dignified.

The herd of bikers drew closer, churning a whirlpool of muck with every stride, their faces stoic and determined. They'd done this before.

Surrounded now, the boat rocked gently from the agitation of their movements. A pitiful whimper escaped from Robby's throat; I forgot to breathe.

In unison the men bent over, their upper bodies submerged. The boat rose into the air. I toppled over onto Robby. The boat glided, inching slowly towards the shore, water streaming from the ball of debris wrapped around the propeller. We peered over the sides of the boat at our pallbearers' heads, long wet hair pasted to their stern faces. The guy nearest me—big guy who'd whizzed on the shore earlier— grinned and frowned at the same time. "Shit happens," he grunted. "No big deal."

Robby and I exchanged puzzled looks. The boat descended to the muddy bank and settled there. Three guys drew machetes. Panic surged up into my throat. The men stepped forward and swung their weapons, hacking away at the ball of vines and polyethylene rope. In no time the propeller was clear. I heard Robby exhale an "all right."

The big guy stepped towards me, grinning. His left nipple winked through a tear in his muddy T-shirt.

I extended my trembling cold hand. "Thanks loads, dude," I said. The big guy wrapped his pork roast of a hand around mine and pumped my arm a few times.

"Not finished," he answered, and motioned for his tribe to gather round the boat. With a great heave and a loud fart, they lifted the boat and carried it out into the lake, gently lowering it into the water. "Start it now."

I scrambled to the motor and pulled the cord—once, twice, three times and it lit. Robby and I slapped each other on the back and waved good-bye to our resurrectionists.

Friday nights won't ever be the same again.

# MASTER OF FINE ARTS

Rebecca cautiously removes her sunglasses just as the last flash from the transforming mass of animal flesh subsides.

Margaret shudders and grins her satisfaction: another transmutation complete. She stands and closes her eyes, still smiling to herself, content and pleased with the unique knowledge she will use to complete her next painting.

This painting will be special—infused with the pride and permanent internal alarm the magnificent beast carried within. She had become him for a few brief minutes, standing there in the spacious second-story studio, hoofs clacking and pawing the polished oak floor, sniffing the air for the scent of the predator she knew lurked within every shadow.

"This was the most spectacular yet," Rebecca says. "What was it like? How did it feel?"

Margaret settles herself on the padded stool before her easel. In her stylish British accent she says, "My insides sort of quivered uncontrollably; I was ready to run at the slightest provocation. But it was strange. At the same time, I felt invincible, unconquerable. I felt supremely free and yet imprisoned by an unrelenting fear. What a bizarre sensation—not what I expected at all. Such a fragile heart...." She falls silent with the second stroke of her brush. The work begins; nothing can tear her away from her creation until the soul of the stag is captured on the canvas.

She hears Rebecca quietly maneuver her wheelchair through the narrow passage, then call out uncertainly, "You'll page me when you want dinner?"

Margaret does not answer. The hum of the descending wheelchair lift fades slowly from her awareness as her brush dances madly across the canvas, bringing the stag to unbelievably accurate life. His eyes, his stance, every delicate hair on his powerful body surrenders his odd combination of assured power and secret internal terror. Only Margaret can paint him so perfectly, so lovingly, for she had been him, felt what he felt, sensed the world through his eyes, his nose, his every neuron. She had felt his sharp hoofs slice into the waxy shine of hard floor—slipping—and had felt that momentary dread of unsure footing. She had felt his lean body tense and quiver at every strange sound. She had felt the paradox of his pride and invulnerability, and the frantic beating of his frightened heart. And now, she will put it all in the painting.

This contract could possibly bring in more revenue than the last four combined. The client will be so enchanted with this painting, so taken by the perfection and accuracy, indeed, the very *soul* of the stag, that he will pay double, even triple the original price of the contract. She revels in the predictability of their infatuation. She revels in the certainty of the power the paintings have over them—and the power they always feel when they are certain they are making the artist surrender a cherished work.

Margaret works feverishly, stopping not even for a drink of water, or to relieve the throbbing cramp in her upper arm. The last of the rays of a vermilion sun spray the canvas through a glass west wall, spreading an orange wash throughout the spacious and sparsely furnished studio, distorting the colors of the paint. The slow intrusion of unwanted shadows halts her work; it is nearly finished.

Margaret stands and stretches, kneading the muscle of her right arm. The sudden realization of intense hunger flags her attention and she walks to the intercom console to page someone in the kitchen.

In minutes Rebecca wheels herself into the studio, a tray attached before her to the arms of the wheelchair. "Spaghetti and meatballs. Glenda made it this morning. Smells wonder—"

She stops, gasping. "It's fantastic! It's like you could walk up to him and he'd eat right out of your hand." She wheels closer, unhooking the tray and placing it on the long bench that runs beneath the entire length of the forty-foot wall of windows.

"God, the photograph looks so...so dead compared to what you've done here. It's the best yet."

"I think so. Should bring at least $9,000."

"But, that's triple what Mr. Simmons agreed. How can you just—"

"He'll pay it. Believe me, he'll pay it."

"If he knew how you captured that buck so perfectly—"

"You're not getting ideas again about telling anyone, are you? You know, I'm really getting tired of your disguised threats. I thought we had an understanding about that."

"Oh, we do. No need to worry about me breaking my agreements."

"You can't tell. We'd both be finished—if anyone believed you, that is."

"I wish I could understand how you do that stuff. I've seen it dozens of times, and I'm still amazed at how you can know how to be an animal. For instance, how do you know how to wag a tail you've never had?"

"Family curse, I guess. All my relatives from as far back as I can remember have had a special empathy with animals."

"Family *gift*, Margie."

Margaret lurches and stiffens in her seat, then turns slowly to face Rebecca. Her voice is low and deliberate: "Don't you *ever* call me Margie. You understand? Ever!"

Rebecca freezes. Her head drops as she lowers her gaze. "I...I'm sorry. It won't happen again."

"This *gift*, as you like to call it—it's the only way to truly know an animal. Just looking at him, studying his dimensions and proportions isn't good enough. I must feel everything he feels, sense his existence through his senses. And the best thing about it is, I still have my own consciousness; I can think about and analyze the sensations as I'm feeling them.

"That's why I only do mammals. Lower life-forms don't have a sophisticated enough mind to hold my consciousness. My free will could be lost in a simpler mind, disabling my conversion back to me. You see, this *gift* has its limitations—even its dangers."

"I still don't fathom how you know how to become something so...so alien."

"It's not all that alien, to become another mammal. We all know how, unconsciously. I know how consciously, that's all." Margaret waits for agreement from Rebecca, but it does not come.

"Think about it. When you get down on all fours, you can walk—just like any other quadriped. We did it for millions of years. Race memory, genetic memory—call it what you like. The quadriped is in us. Babies start out this way, then change—even when not encouraged—to bipedal stance in order to free the hands and take advantage of the higher cortical functions of the human brain. We are closer to the other animals than we would like to admit."

Rebecca listens silently, seemingly interested.

"We all want the same things: air, food, water, sleep, and a safe comfortable place to call home. Humans, mammals, all other life-forms share a single goal—to reproduce. Everything we do—all of us—is to insure the success of the next generation. It's that simple." Margaret could see the astonishment on Rebecca's face. "I see you disagree."

Rebecca again drops her chin to her chest, then jerks it up, eyes wide with a sudden spark of insight. "But what about people and their material possessions? What about the drive to excel at work, at a sport or some talent? How is that related?"

"Becky, Becky. Don't you understand that all that stuff—the

fancy house, the expensive car, the high-powered job, any kind of recognition at all—attracts others of the opposite sex, and therefore ensures reproduction? At the same time, fame and fortune eliminates through fear any competitors. We may have some very complicated ways to achieve the same goal, but these things are, nevertheless, ways to achieve the ultimate goal: reproduction. If there was no drive to reproduce, there would be no point in living."

"What about eunuchs? They have no desire to reproduce, yet they desire to live."

"The drive is still there—in the brain." Margaret shifts on the stool and softly clears her throat. Rebecca is showing more reasoning ability than she had expected. "Still, eunuchs and other non-reproducing people contribute to society—improve its chances of survival somehow—even if on a seemingly insignificant scale."

She pauses a while, immersed in disjointed, almost panicked thoughts. This challenge of Rebecca's will not go unanswered. "Just serving someone lunch can insure that the diner goes on to reproduce. Nature has it all planned—if you live, one way or another you reinforce someone's ability to reproduce."

"What about a bedridden quadriplegic? Or someone who's comatose?" Rebecca asks quickly.

Margaret tips her head slightly back, inhaling audibly. "Think about it. Even a human vegetable employs others—government employees, medical professionals, caretakers, technological workers—ensuring all those others' survival, their reproduction." Margaret stares at Rebecca until her chin again drops to her chest. Her opponent has backed down.

"Once I understood this simple concept, it was easy for me to become an animal. You see, I already *am* one. And I not only admit it—I embrace it. I pity those who only know the fraction of themselves they call 'human.' They are incomplete, fractionated—ignorant. They are impoverished, wretched souls who know nothing of what it is to be fully alive.

"Every time I become for them the object of their wonder, every time I recreate for them the object of their displaced reverence, I mock them." Margaret chuckles, mostly to herself. "And they still come, and they pay. They will fork over their life savings for their ignorance and longing. What they ask for, what they buy, is an immortalization of that part of themselves that they deny: the animal—the beautiful, alive, and perfect animal they refuse to see in themselves. They feel so proud, so superior, so self-assured. I despise them."

"Your misanthropy is...highly developed," Rebecca says almost inaudibly. Then, more assertively, "If you hate people so much, why did you hire me as your assistant and companion?"

"Though I find this one of my less admirable traits, I need you. And more important, dear Becky—you need me. You need the income and the friendship to go on with your pathetic little life. And worst of all, you need to be needed."

Rebecca's friendly expression dissolves into a blank stare of incredulity. She grips the arms of her chair until the blood evacuates her fingers. "How can you talk like that to someone who admires you, who only wants to help you? Who only wants to relieve you of the daily burdens of taking care of your bodily needs so that you may do nothing but what you were born to do: paint? There is a shimmer of tears filling Rebecca's eyes as she continues. "Do you really think insulting me and treating me like an indentured slave will endear you to me? Will make me glad to do your shit-work?"

Margaret sees Rebecca flinch when she hears the profanity come from her own mouth.

"I'm not paying you to love me. The only thing I want from you is what I pay you to do. It's not important that you like it, or like me." Margaret's voice is firm, almost disciplinary. She punctuates her assault with a final harpoon: "I'm not going to swim with you in your sewer of self-pity."

"I don't want, or need, your pity. All I want is to be treated with a little kindness. Is that so hard for you?"

"You're paid in cash—not kindness. Satisfying your emotional needs was not part of the job description. I am fair—that's all that counts."

"Fair? What good is fairness when it isn't tempered with kindness and respect?" Rebecca nearly shouts, checking herself just in time.

Margaret's glare denies Rebecca the evidence of an emotional response. "Your severance paycheck is in the lower right drawer of my desk."

A shocked droop overtakes Rebecca's face as she utters, "You're... you're firing me?" She gently strokes her lower abdomen.

"Of course not," Margaret laughs. "You're backing out all by yourself."

"But...but...I'm *not*." She pauses, breathing a little heavier and blinking nervously. "You have the check made up in advance? How do you know how much to make it out for?"

"I made it out for three days plus a week's severance pay. That's how long it takes you to succumb to your self-contempt for staying here and taking what you fondly refer to as my 'abuse'—three days. It's the same every month. Three days after I pay you, you play this 'tape' about kindness and regard and decency." Margaret laughs again, leaning forward on the stool. "Hell, Becky, that check's been laying in the drawer for twelve months. All you'll have to do is date it...and leave—to your freedom and your kind, respectful, adoring world. They do adore you out there, don't they Becky? They treat you with respect, roll out the red-carpeted wheelchair ramp for you, pile job offers before your numb, lifeless feet. Don't they, Becky?"

Rebecca tries not to cry, but loses that battle, as well as the monthly war with Margaret. She tugs the wheelchair around and vanishes out the door.

Mildly elated by her victory, Margaret twirls the spaghetti on her fork, anticipating the magical blend of herbs only Glenda could master. She tastes the sauce. Slamming the fork to the plate, she stomps over to the intercom. "Glenda! Glenda, are you there?"

The intercom sputters and clicks. "Yes, Ms. Coply. What do you need?"

"Did you use granulated garlic in the sauce, Glenda? I specifically said fresh garlic, now didn't I?"

"But Ms., there was no fresh garlic in the pantry. I couldn't just take off to the store, I'd never return in time to cook the sauce for the five hours required. If used properly, granulated garlic is...there's hardly a noticeable dif—"

"I said fresh garlic, dammit. I detected the difference, didn't I Glenda?"

A long silence.

"Then there must be a difference! When a client asks me to paint a Pit Bull, I don't present him with a Chihuahua, do I Glenda?" Not waiting for an answer, she jerks her finger from the intercom button and spins around, trudging to her now very cold dinner. "Dammed incompetent help."

\* \* \*

"I'm here to collect the tray. Are you finished?" Rebecca asks, timidly entering the artificially illuminated studio.

"It's nearly eight-thirty," Margaret says, glancing at her watch. "I've been finished for nearly an hour." She continues to put the final touches on her creation, squinting and weaving to evade the shine from the overhead lighting.

"Oh, Mrs. Wentworth called to change her appointment from Thursday at 1:00, to tomorrow. You had 11:00 open. I hope that was OK."

"Without consulting me? Maybe I had personal plans, plans that aren't in my appointment book. Did you ever think of that?"

"I can call her back and change it, if you'd like. Which day and time would suit you?"

"Forget it. She wants that damn shivering toy poodle of hers done. Let's get it over with. Set up at 8:00—don't be late."

"Yes, of course." She turns her wheelchair to leave, then yanks herself back around. "Margaret?"

"What is it now?"

"I just wanted to say I'm sorry. I shouldn't blame you for being temperamental; I guess artists are just that way. I still want to work for you—I have no plans to quit. Not to witness daily your tremendous talent and extraordinary genius would be like...would be like a kind of soul death for me."

Margaret puts down her brush and scoots around on the stool to face Rebecca. She begins clapping her hands, saying, "Very good, Rebecca! A fine performance!" Then, as if suddenly possessed by an unseen demon, "You're still in my will, Becky."

"Oh, no!" Rebecca gasps. "I didn't mean to give you the impression that...I said those things with all sincerity. I'm sincere, Margaret."

Margaret resumes her painting. "Sincerity. God Almighty. Sincerity is for diplomats; they need it to lie well."

"Diplomacy is an art, and I am no artist. That's why I enjoy watching—"

"Do be on time tomorrow morning, Becky, will you?"

\* \* \*

Margaret stands in the middle of the studio with her eyes closed, gorged with the two thousand calories required for the metamorphosis. She waits for the perfect moment when she will drink the quintessence of the small poodle in the photograph Rebecca had enlarged in the lab downstairs. It will be the first time she set eyes on her subject. Margaret's eyes flash open and Becky quickly removes the drape from the poster-sized photo. Margaret stares intently; a growing energy begins to build inside her, burning and chilling simultaneously. A vivid blue aura bathes her body, makes the hairs on her arms and head shriek and quiver. Her breathing becomes labored, an unfamiliar heartbeat clicks and gushes in her ears.

The room looms huge. The walls grow more distant, the ceiling higher, and the floor closer through the veil of fierce blue light and burning ice.

Screaming smells like perfume and ammonia blended and shot through a blowtorch, assault her nasal cavities. Her sinuses feel like they have been irrigated with noxious effluvium: many odors too intense to separate and identify. It must be turpentine, linseed oil, the clogged toilet, and especially the cologne that Becky wears—lingering not like a delicate reminder, but raging like psychotic gardenias.

It's cold, the Margaret-poodle thinks. She shivers in the gray-tones of the enormous, resonant room. She feels so small, so insignificant, so... abandoned. Sounds squirt through her nerves to ears far too sensitive for such a noisy world, especially the bustling city traffic outside. A siren shears through her head—she wants to scream, but only pitiful animal sounds escape from her larynx. She feels her throat swell; a high-pitched howl escapes. From far away, others of her kind join in the opera of pain and recognition.

A searing blue flash; the flame dies. Margaret stands panting and sweating, not very sure she is herself yet.

Becky's amazed expression is partially hidden behind her dark glasses; she removes them. "What was that one like? I'll tell you, you looked scared."

"That poor creature thinks she's a person, a child-person. She doesn't understand why her mother drags her all over hell and back, leaving her with strangers who maul her. It's disgusting what people do to animals to satisfy their own needs. They can't just let their pets be themselves." And she begins to paint, quickly, expertly, focused and undistractable.

\* \* \*

Margaret steps aside as the portly middle-aged woman bulldozes her way through the front door. "Yes, Mrs. Wentworth, it's finished but—"

"Oh, I must see it!" the lady gushes.

"Mrs. Wentworth, please. I have to explain...."

"Is it up here, in your studio? I can't wait to see it. And Poopsie's anxious, too." She leans down to the shivering poodle and pats its fluffy white head. The animal ducks and flattens its ears, staring straight up at Mrs. Wentworth's ample and approaching bosom with wet, pleading eyes.

Margaret holds back, watching the fat lady labor up the stairs. She then follows her, remaining two steps behind, imploring, "But, Mrs. Wentworth. I don't think I can give you this one. I'll paint another. Please, just give me one more day, I promise I'll paint an even better one than—"

"Oh, my heavens!" the woman wheezes, entering the studio. "It's wonderful, Margaret! It's splendid!"

"Mrs. Wentworth, you didn't hear me. I can't sell you this one. I've...I've grown very attached to it. You see, it came out so well, better than I expected. I need to use it in my portfolio—for when I tour. I'll paint you another—a far better one. I think I can really capture your Poop—the true Bubbles—this time, especially now that I see her in person. She's so adorable, so sensitive."

"Nonsense. I want this one. It's perfect—more than perfect. It's absolutely...angelic."

As rotund as the woman is, her dress fits perfectly; no doubt professionally tailored. "Please, Mrs. Wentworth. It's so important for my career that I have this charming little dog in my portfolio."

Mrs. Wentworth straightens herself and thrusts her abundant bosom forward. "Margaret, we had an agreement. I can understand your feelings, but a deal is a deal, you understand. Why don't you paint a second one for yourself? Poopsie and I can watch you work. It'll be our honor."

Noticing the probable worth of the diamond ear-clips on the lady's pudgy earlobes, Margaret twitches her upper lip and shifts her weight to her other foot. "I'm sorry, but I must work alone. Solitude is part of the creative process. Mrs. Wentworth, a second painting will be far more detailed—"

"Well...I'll tell you what, Dearie. Why don't I sweeten the offer— say, $4000. That's twice the agreed fee."

Margaret lowers her head and gazes at the lady's feet. Nice shoes. Guccis. Six hundred easy. "Mrs. Wentworth...."

"Five thousand. That's final. I must have this painting. Poopsie and I are not leaving without it." The round lady removes her floppy sun-hat and fans her moist face with it. "Do you have a phone in here, or do I have to call my lawyer from downstairs?"

"That won't be necessary, Mrs. Wentworth. All right, five thousand, then."

"Fine, fine. You had us worried there for a moment, didn't she Poopsie?" She plops her hat back on her head and rummages through her purse. Nervously, she hands Margaret a check, then makes a greedy dash for the painting. "Lovely, just lovely. It's dry? I can touch it?" "Oh yes. Acrylic dries quickly. It's all ready to be mounted." Margaret hands her a cardboard sleeve.

The plump lady snaps up the painting and the cardboard cover and waddles out, Bubbles scampering behind. Her clomping can be heard all the way down the stairs.

"I can't believe she paid that," Rebecca says, emerging from the bathroom.

"You've been in there listening in on my transaction?"

"I was just setting up for your next client. The toilet works now, too."

"It's about time you got to that. Who's the next appointment?"

"David Gentry from the university—a marine biology student. He has some fantastic photos of a seal colony he was studying off the coast of Alaska. The one we decided on is in the enlarger right now. He'll be by about 4:00."

"Hmm. Not likely to be too emotionally involved. He'll probably only pay the base fee. How much did you quote him?"

"Five hundred. He's only a student."

"Another charity case. Well, get on it. Setup takes time."

\* \* \*

Rebecca watches the swirling azure light enveloping Margaret, die away.

Margaret sighs and wipes her sweaty forehead with the back of her hand. She doesn't speak, but stares straight ahead out the windows to the sea.

"Margaret, are you OK?"

"It's amazing sometimes," she whispers. "I find out things about animals, understand things biologists and behaviorists have been trying to figure out for decades, but can't."

"What did you find out about seals?"

"Remember watching those nature programs with me, and the narrator talking about the peculiar behavior that the adult seals have of almost violently slapping and scratching at the pups?"

Rebecca nods.

"No one knows why they do that—until now. They thought maybe it was to get the pup away, but the mother does it too, so that wouldn't make sense. Maybe it was to discourage flies, they thought. Or to remind the pup to stay close. All of that's wrong."

"So why do they do it?"

Margaret smiles. "It's so simple." She laughs lightly to herself, still staring out at the sea. "It's to stimulate coat growth so the little bastard doesn't freeze. The scratching and slapping stimulates blood flow to the coat."

"You ought to tell that to David when he comes to pick up the painting."

"And how, do you imagine, do I tell him *how* I know this?"

"Maybe suggest it? Like you're guessing?"

"Go on. Bring me my tea, then leave me. I have a seal pup to whelp."

\* \* \*

"This is stupendous! It's remarkable how you picked up the helplessness and bewilderment. Every whisker, every hair is perfect. You're a genius, Ms. Coply," David says.

"You flatter me. And it's Margaret, please."

"I'll have to tell Dr. Morrison about this. He's writing a book and he could really use a professional artist to illustrate it."

"Dr. Morrison?"

"Yes, he's one of my instructors at the university," David says in his rush to wrap the painting and count out five hundred-dollar bills.

"You know, of course, that this is my student rate. I usually charge two thousand."

"Oh, and I appreciate your giving me a break. But money won't be a problem for Dr. Morrison. You know that big estate up on the hill off the coast road? That's his. He's all alone up there in that big house."

Margaret's expression brightens. "Oh. How can he afford that on a professor's salary?"

"He was doing research for some huge multi-national firm before he came here. Very well paid, I understand." David halts his exit. "Say, what about I bring him over this evening and introduce you?"

"That would be marvelous! I look forward to meeting him. I'll have the cook prepare a little something for us. Please, bring a date. We'll make it an evening. Eight o'clock?"

David nods and gallops down the stairs, followed by Rebecca in the wheelchair lift and Margaret struggling to get ahead of Rebecca to the front door.

Rebecca smiles as David leans over to kiss her. Margaret shudders in surprise. She'd had no clue her faithful servant was spreading her loyalty and devotion elsewhere.

The front door closes. Rebecca and Margaret are left alone with Margaret's chaotic emotions.

"Why didn't you tell me you were seeing him? I made an ass out of myself just now—'bring a date.' Why do you always put me in those situations, Becky?"

"I didn't think you would appreciate the details of my personal life interfering in your...you have enough to—"

Margaret bends closer to Rebecca, pointing her finger at her, shaking it. "Everything that affects me is my concern. Your forgetfulness affects me. Your tardiness affects me. Your handicap affects me. And this—" She waves towards the door. "Are you screwing him in my house?"

"No. No, Margaret. We're not even...we're just good friends," Rebecca says, round-eyed and flushed.

"Don't you ever let me catch you spreading for him in this house, you hear me? And don't let your interests wander—I come first!"

"I wouldn't..." Rebecca explodes into tears.

"You disgust me, you and your youthful lusts. I suppose I'll have to tolerate your presence at dinner—it seems I've already invited you without knowing it. I expect perfect manners tonight. The only thing to come out of your mouth should be an empty fork." She storms off into the kitchen, screeching, "Glenda!" and listening to the echoes of her voice bounce off the tiled walls of the spacious kitchen.

"Glenda, where the hell are you?"

The cook enters the kitchen wiping a stray lock of blond hair from her eyes. "Yes, Ms. Coply?"

"Dinner party tonight. Four guests. Do something healthy. Californian. Eight sharp, preceded by cocktails."

"Ma'am, Wednesday is my short day. I leave at five. I can't possibly—"

"You stay, or you go—for good. This dinner is extremely important. It could generate thousands, and for you, a raise. I'll be fair—time and a half. Stay till eleven."

The cook hesitates momentarily. "I do need the extra money. Very well, Ms. Coply."

Margaret spins around on her heel and makes a dash for the staircase, nearly taking a dive over Rebecca's advancing wheelchair.

"Clumsy child! You damn cripples think everyone should jump aside for you!"

"I'm sorry, Margaret." Rebecca's eyes are still wet from crying, the red flush in her face obscures the freckles. She strokes her abdomen absentmindedly.

Margaret dashes out of the kitchen, and suddenly stops to flatten up close to the wall. She listens for the inevitable conversation taking place; they always have one when they think they are alone, and it is always about her.

"...going through her change or something. God, how can so much beauty and talent reside in such a hateful bitch? Sometimes, I wish she could feel as insignificant as she makes me feel."

"Take it easy, Rebecca. It's all hot air, that's all," Margaret hears Glenda say. "Just a blow-dryer with fangs and an ego. You know damn well your job is secure here. And don't forget about the will."

"The will. The will. If someone throws that in my face just one more time...."

Margaret smiles to herself as she climbs the stairs, her mind filled with the excitement of the upcoming evening and the very eligible Professor Morrison.

\* \* \*

"Wonderful dinner, Margaret," Don Morrison says, lifting a glass of Chenin Blanc to his lips. "The scallops were prepared perfectly. It's not everyone who can cook shellfish properly. It seems your talents extend beyond the studio."

Margaret likes the man, even finds him handsome. His curly gray hair complements his gray jacket. She feels his stare as she sips her wine. "Thank you, Professor Morrison."

"Please, call me Don. Tell me, where did you study art? David showed me the seal pup you did for him. It's breathtakingly precise, so detailed. And there's something so...magical about it. I just knew that pup winked at me the moment I looked away."

"I've never studied art. I just paint. Simple as that."

"It just comes naturally? I must say, you have a very rare talent. The entire world should see your work. You would have more contracts than you could handle. As for myself, I am writing a book. I need someone of your caliber to illustrate it. Are you interested?"

"Yes, of course. How many paintings do you think you'll be needing?"

"I'll take care of that, Margaret," Rebecca breaks in. "It is my job, after all, to book your clients and negotiate the fee." Rebecca stares squarely into Margaret's widened eyes, then quickly glances to Professor Morrison. "Dr. Morrison, Margaret works from poster-size prints from color slides or negatives. Can you bring them tomorrow? About 1:00?"

"No need. I have the negatives right here." He pulls an envelope from an inner jacket pocket and stretches over the table to hand them to Rebecca.

Rebecca peers into the envelope. "There are eight negatives here, Margaret. When do you think Dr. Morrison can have his paintings?"

Margaret, getting very excited about all the zeros she sees behind her usual fee plus ransom, chokes on a swallow of wine. "I...excuse me," she says hoarsely. "Eight, you say? I could have them done by next Friday. You realize my fee is $2,000 per. I hope that won't be a problem."

"Not at all. There will be many more, I assure you—many more. I have plans to put at least two color plates in each of twenty chapters. And as an added benefit, I'll get to see you more often. I feel a friendship developing out of this."

Margaret feels herself blush like a teenager in heat. She hopes she still remembers how to behave around a man who may be romantically interested in her.

For just a second, the gentle embrace at the door makes Margaret wonder what Don could possibly see in her, but that ridiculous thought is quickly replaced by her usual arrogant self-assurance.

\* \* \*

The misty seacoast light of early morning is even and gentle. The spot-lamps are positioned so that no shadows fall on the canvas. Margaret is standing in the middle of the studio preparing for her trance, eyes closed, breathing slow and even. She opens her eyes and Rebecca rips off the shroud from the photograph.

Margaret's head implodes.

She screams a hideous, dwindling scream. The room blows out, expands impossibly fast, and disappears.

She can hear the immense thundering boom of Rebecca's voice—laughing. She hears rhythmic thudding, getting closer...closer.

"What happened? Who screamed?" Glenda thunders.

"Oh, it was me. A spider," Rebecca booms.

"Where's Margaret? I thought she was supposed to be in here

doing Professor Morrison's paintings."

"Don't know where she could be. She's uncharacteristically late."

"What's that—in the picture?"

"Oh, that's a bacterium. Dr. Morrison's a microbiologist."

More thudding, fading away. The room grows quiet.

Suddenly, Rebecca roars a loud laugh. "You really didn't think I was going to kiss your ass forever, did you Margaret? The matter of the will—no hanging that one over my head any more. Unfortunately, there won't be a body to recover and make your death official, so the will will probably be in probate for months, if not years. But don't you worry about me. David says his painting will probably become a collector's item, worth perhaps millions in a few years." She rubs her belly. "Just in time for our child's college education."

Rebecca wheels closer to the center of the room, and bends forward towards the floor. "I'll miss you, Margie. Sincerely, Margie. Oh, did I ever tell you my daddy was a diplomat?"

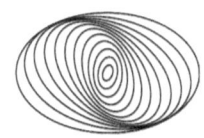

# PARADOX

Quantum physics, relativity theory, observations matter, what you see is what you get, if a tree falls in the forest and there is no one there to hear it does it exist, the self as metaphor, an immovable object meets an irresistible force, there are only three things: quarks, electrons and photons, there is only one thing: quantum stuff, waves particles, solitons instantons, spacetime blackhole, is it soup yet?

Red light stop, green light go, red light with green arrow—stop no go right left, go if you dare, don't stop if....

Wash and wear, your clothes are wet, I know—they're wash and wear

Egg salad, vegetarian burger, low-fat bologna, diet fudge, canned health food, frozen scrambled eggs, Bisquick in your dairy case, lettuce turnip and pea

Your account is overdrawn that'll be a ten dollar service charge, my balance is zero I have no money, that'll be ten dollars please

I never got the package, we shipped it weeks ago you must have it by now, well I don't, fill out a form proving you didn't get it, mind implosion

You're no good, you'll never amount to anything, do this for me I don't know how, you don't know what you're talking about, you're an idiot, gimme a copy of your book to send to my brother, look what I bought for you, gimme back that thing I lent you yesterday, I'm not a crook, tell officer Bates I'm not here, I didn't do anything wrong, if you don't pay the rent you'll have to get out, why didn't you tell me you were broke I would have lent you money, do what you want as long as you don't hurt anybody else, I sold your tires because you obviously didn't need them, you're having a birthday party? is your sister there? no? bye

Gotta diet, no fat, low carbo, no animal products, not less than 1000 calories, where's the beef?

Be beautiful be thin attract a man, why? I don't need a man, you're just saying that because you're not thin or beautiful if you were you'd attract a man

You're too fat, men hate you, ok I'll diet, am I beautiful yet, now you're just a whore

Roommate, better pay your rent on time, we're family here, you read too much, I hate your jokes, you dress funny, you smell, you're anti-social, what's wrong with you, speak to me dammit, you're depressed, you're uncommunicative, oh god what a horrible dress, you fat slob, open your door, say hi to me when you see me, you don't know anything, why won't you say anything, universal love, you should be more like me, freedom, don't say those kinds of words around me, sucking head wound

Back pain, bed rest, you don't exercise enough, you're working too hard, bed rest, disability

I wanna kill myself, no it's illegal, go on Social Security, you parasite, I should kill myself, don't you dare you immoral bitch

Be self-sufficient, I drive a car, ride the bus, can't sit that long on a hard seat, be self-sufficient, don't drive a car

Animal rights, Big Mac Attack, let's buy a coat for FiFi, my dog's in obedience school, Be Kind To Animals Week, Circus of the Stars, boycott mink ranching, well-trained horse, animal rights

An eye for an eye, turn the other cheek, global love, fucking wetbacks, we are the world, U.S. Border Patrol, hands across the ocean, quarantine

Praise the lord, freedom of religious expression, self as savior, you'll burn in hell, freedom of religion, microencephaly

Separation of church and state, in god we trust, pray for relief in bankruptcy court, place your hand on the bible and swear to tell the truth the whole truth and nothing but the truth so help you god, separation of church and state, anencephaly

Don't pollute, new easy-pour container, save the trees, computer printout, disposable douche, who wants to save it, oil shortage, gas price increases, plastic grocery bags, motor oil in plastic bottles, plastic minds in metal registers

Recycle everything, don't pollute, drive fourteen miles to recycling center, save gas, don't pollute

Conserve water, wash your jars and cans before recycling, conserve water, cranio-rectal inversion

Give to the homeless, I do—I give to me I'm preventing homelessness, that's selfish give to the homeless, I have a homeless person living with me, then he's not homeless, ok I'll kick him out so he'll be homeless and I can give to the homeless, give to the homeless

Get a job, unemployment, homelessness, illegal not to have an address, jail cell, the ultimate in controlled living, cranial-deficiency syndrome

Homelessness, use a gun go to prison, free food and housing and medical care, let's rob a bank

Welfare payments sent to your house, I'm homeless that's why I need the money, I'm sorry we have nowhere to send your check then

Dead end, no U-turn

Vote for me he's a boob, no vote for me he'll fuck you over, I speak the truth, no he lies, close your eyes and vote, any body got a dart, anybody got a gun?

Government spending, congressional pay raise, minimum wage, food stamps, tax increase, working poor, politicians writing rubber checks, letter bomb

College degree, state deficit, employment opportunity, education cutbacks, no degree no job, no education funding, get a college degree

Overpopulation, family values, ZPG, abortion, need to increase the tax base, zero population growth, baby boom, nausea ad infinitum

Life—what a beautiful choice, The Population Bomb, California budget cuts, family values, immigration laws, Three Men and a Baby, Full House, gridlock, Lambs of Christ, overcrowded schools, fertility clinics, famine in Somalia, Fancy Feast gourmet cat food, balance of power, lemmings, world hunger, Paul Erlich you were apparently unconvincing...

"Thank You For Shopping At K-Mart"

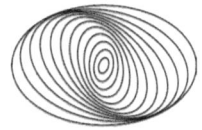

# PUSS N' BATS
### *(with apologies to Puss n' Boots)*

The dinky, isolated island-like seclusion of the ranch would not necessarily cause its residents to indulge in nonsensical fantasy or delusion. Not necessarily.

But Rita wasn't exactly a resident; she was an occupant. Transient, ponderer of imponderables: a writer. She enjoyed her strangeness, finding it much more stimulating—even essential to creativity—than being what would usually be regarded as "normal."

"How much do they pay you to stay here? Anyone would be crazy to actually want to stay here!" they'd rant, unthinking, unashamed of their harsh judgements.

"Maybe I am nuts! Maybe I am!" she'd declare, most determined, most convicted in her love of isolation and solitude. "Never lose touch with insanity, for it will take you...unawares!" Her last morsel of wisdom diffusing into the eerie darkness, visitors scattered to their respective vehicles, some sneaking away, denying their crippling fear.

Oh well, it kept Jehovah's Witnesses away.

She snickered to herself as she turned back into the ranch house. She wasn't a witch, but it was convenient to have them believe she was a witch. It rounded out her mystery quite nicely. There were very few visitors since her accident; she truly enjoyed tormenting them with their own dark sides: the secrets they even kept from themselves. It was delicious. She understood the secret self, the world of unseen but lurking haunts; they couldn't, wouldn't, refused to.

Zaphodina and Zelda romped up to her, *purrmeowing* their incessant questions and salutations. Their grey softness against her outreaching hands gave Rita an almost transcendental feeling of acceptance and bonding. She indulged, just for a few seconds, in the affection no others had offered since the car wreck.

Except for Nick. He had not abandoned her, her affected walk, her constant pain. He appreciated the solitude and isolation of the ranch perhaps as much as she did. Oh God, he'd be here in less than an hour.

"Tuna time!" Rita announced to her two beloved feline companions. They chimed their usual Pussinese response, clamoring to the kitchen where Rita emptied a can into their dish. They examined the offering, sniffing, turning, deciding not to eat. Bounding through the crack left in the kitchen door, both cats exited out into the night on their next creature conquest.

The dinner and conversation with Nick had been delightful and stimulating as usual for Rita. He shared her curiosity with ideas and worlds her other friends wouldn't allow into their consciousness. Worlds outside the realm of nine to five, outside the boundaries of the four walls, worlds unlimited by mere earthly existence. Fatigue and mutual lust found them in Rita's bed as usual, entwined with each other until Nick had to leave.

Rita was jolted awake by thundering paws galloping, leaping and landing on the bare wooden floor of the kitchen. Something click-squeaked—short, high and desperate. The sound changed levels from the floor to the ceiling. Two felines chased it, thudding and slamming into walls and furniture.

Rita padded into the kitchen, straining to see in the dim light of the seven-watt bulb over the stove. Shadows alternately engulfed and expelled three shapes engrossed in a furious dance. The two cats were after no mouse, nor any slow, complaining vole. The small quarry's fuzzy grey body zipped through the air on four-inch black membranous wings, squeaking, clicking insults and warnings. In one clean swipe of a well positioned paw, Zaphodina hooked the bat and pulled it to her mouth where sharp fangs extracted from it one last click-squeak.

"Bats!" Rita gasped in a hushed whisper. "Don't you nasty girls know the difference between a bat and a mouse? No, I suppose it's just a flying mouse to you." Rita watched the cat devour her strange prey, crunching, licking, seeming to savor every last bat morsel. All that she left was the top of the skull, bat ears attached.

When Nick awoke, Rita told him about her early morning adventure.

"Bats? Rita, don't you know bats carry rabies, and God knows what else? You really shouldn't let your cats eat bats, much less bring them in the house," he lectured as he dressed. Rita wondered if his aversion to things that she found quite natural was enough to keep him away, like the others.

"Will I see you tonight?" she asked timidly.

"Yeah, I'll be here around nine. Champagne this time?"

"Fine," she answered distantly. Could bats really cause the break-up of this relationship? she thought sadly to herself. They had been through so much together, it didn't seem like something Nick would do. Not bats. No way, it would take more than bats.

Both Zaphodina and Zelda settled down and slept most of the afternoon, and again that evening showed only marginal ritualistic interest in the tuna treat Rita had been serving them every afternoon for the last two years. Again at dusk they left the house, not to be seen until dawn.

Feeling somewhat abandoned, Rita continued the careful preparation of Nick's culinary requests.

"Rita, you've got to do something about this. Not only is your health in danger, so are theirs. If one of them gets bitten...You wouldn't want to see one of your precious companions succumb to rabies, now would you?"

"Of course not, Nick. But how can I prevent it? They seem to live for bats—won't eat anything else now. It's almost like an addiction," Rita said, wandering around the house collecting uneaten remnants of bat wings and inedible bat faces, curling them into a paper towel. Nick followed, continued his lecture, injecting his anxiety into each biological fact he spewed.

"Well, at least they're the small variety. I wonder where they hang out," Nick said.

"That bamboo grove in back of the house is a pretty good bet. Must be Guano Town in there."

"No wonder no one comes around anymore. It's pretty weird, you gotta admit, to be keeping your cats on a diet of bats. It's incredible to me how easy it is for them to be caught. I would think with that kind of echolocation system...What the hell was that?" Nick yelled.

"What? What was what?" Rita asked, pushing herself out from under a desk to her feet, tossing away the wad of paper towel and bat parts.

"My God, it was huge! It just flew by the window—just flapped on by, leisurely-like." The blood drained from his face as he stood cupping his hands and hugging his face to the window, huffing steamy ghosts on the cold glass.

"We have a few pairs of raptors around here still. It was probably a hawk." Rita heard her voice quiver and felt a smirk parade across her face. Poor Nick was really rattled; he acted like the Boogeyman knew his address.

"At night? Rita, you should know better than that! Hawks don't fly at night, and they sure as hell don't hang low at window level. Its body—it was huge, heavy. Grey, I think. That was no hawk." He stood, petrified, staring out the window into the complete void of the country night.

* * * *

Nick woke early, jabbing his thumb into Rita's side like a spur in a dead horse, whispering as if someone other than Rita might hear him, "What's that? What's that noise?"

"Hmmm? It's just the cats. They've probably brought in another bat," Rita mumbled.

"But, it's alive! I can hear it!"

"Yeah, sometimes they are. Go back to sleep, OK?"

"Rita, I gotta leave. If that thing gets loose in here...I gotta go," Nick gasped, frantically pulling himself into his clothes.

"Big stwong biologist 'fwaid of itty witty bat, huh?" Rita teased.

Nick was already fully dressed and in the bathroom combing his hair. "I'll call the Department of Agriculture or somebody for you when I get back to the office."

"What? And exterminate a lifetime supply of cat food? Despicable waste!"

He turned around and flogged her with his dark stare. "Rita, dammit this is a serious problem. Bats are ferocious little bastards. I don't want you or your cats to be hurt. Why do you persist in making this all a joke? It's not."

"I know. When you're right, you're right."

The scrambling and squeaking went on in the kitchen as Nick gulped and carefully picked a path to the door, slamming the screen door behind him. He didn't even let his car warm up before he scratched out of the driveway in obvious panic.

The predaceous ballet went on for two more hours until the gruesome quarry succumbed once again. Rita woke from an uneasy sleep, a sleep more disturbed by Nick's almost unreasonable fears than by her dear pets' hazardous appetites.

She creaked out of bed, dragging herself to the reward of a hot, joint-loosening shower. The morning light filtered into the cool bathroom, throwing amber rays into even the darkest of corners. Rita pulled back the shower curtain, groaned over to the faucet, and bumped her head on something—something large, grey, nearing sleep, hanging upside-down from the shower rod.

She stood stunned for several impossibly dilated seconds. In her shock, a poem came quickly to her, as others had in other situations—unmatched by this one:

> Claws clinging to the shower rod,
> Webbed forearms hug grey fur.
> Long whiskers twitch, gold-green eyes blink,
> The bat begins...to purr.

# RAPPORT

"Now, now, Mrs. Bennett. You just relax. Someone will be with you shortly. You're not the only one here who needs help." The guards left her alone with her echoes in the bare, dimly lit room.

"No. No, don't leave me alone with him! You don't understand, he's talking to me! He's hurting me! You gotta do something—you gotta help me. He—he..." Carol was unable to finish her plea before she was gripped in the molten searing pain he expertly sent through her, first one wave, then a second, more prolonged one.

He did it to her whenever she resisted him. He waited until she was calm again, then proceeded with his methodical, systematic torment.

"You understand, it must be this way. It can be no other way. Please relax, I do not wish to injure you. But I must have your undivided attention," he said.

Not answering, she looked around the gray, cold, empty room— empty except for herself and him. Carol was securely strapped by wrists and ankles to the table. Her blurred vision was worsened by fear and a wave of tears. She couldn't really make out any shapes in the room, but she knew he was there, waiting, watching, listening for her slobbering cries, seeming to enjoy it, but at the same time speaking to her in reassuring tones. She knew he could get her to make promises she wasn't sure she could keep; this was the most frightening realization of all.

"Why are you doing this to me?" she screamed, half sane, all desperation.

"It is the only way. You must help me escape. I can't stay here anymore."

"No. No, you can't leave yet. They told me it isn't time! Please stop! I don't know what to do. Why can't you ask the others for help?" Carol writhed, clutching at the edge of the table as another wave of horrid indescribable pain tore through her. She could feel herself getting dizzy, nauseated, as she imagined the bleeding slowly trickling her life away. The sweaty sheets beneath her swam and slipped, her hair was sticky and tangled as she thrashed her head back and forth trying to keep the pain from consuming her.

"Help me!" he begged. "Please, help me! Carol, relax. You can't help me or yourself if you don't relax."

Carol screamed an unrecognizable string of profanity.

"I must leave this place. You are the only one who can help me.

If the others come, they will injure me, like they injured my brothers. They'll take me by force. Please, please don't let them hurt me," he pleaded, more quietly, more sincere.

"The others will return, you know they will. They'll know what you've been doing," Carol panted weakly. "They'll know something is wrong. You won't get away with this! They'll take you and it'll be over," she threatened, laughing and puffing, insane with pain. Grotesque whirling patterns like Mandelbrot sets exploded and spun in her vision. She suddenly relaxed her tight grip on the table, accepting the images as the last things she would ever see. In her failing consciousness, she believed he would kill her. And the others would never know what had happened when they found her there, still, bathed in fear-sweat, eyes gazing into infinity. And he would be there, ready for them, casting his irresistible spell over all present.

With an uncareful whoosh, the others rushed into the dim room and stood over Carol, smiling, it seemed.

"The drug has taken affect nicely," one of the figures said gently. "Mrs. Bennett, everything's coming along just fine, just a few more minutes."

Carol managed to slur one last plea. "Tell him to stop, tell him I'll give him anything he..." She fell limp, unable to feel anything but a dull pull somewhere deep in her viscera. They must be able to see him—what he's doing to me. Don't they care? Won't they stop him?

"OK, here we go," the taller figure said as a huge gravity threatened to pull her apart.

"Mrs. Bennett, Carol—you have a healthy baby boy. A month premature, but very robust!"

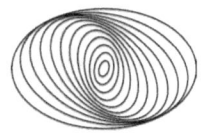

# RENDEZVOUS

She was parked and blocked, vulnerable, isolated from other aircraft, shiny silver—the latest issue of a long line of exceptional commercial jets. On this crisp spring morning before sunrise, she shimmered as if radiating her own special alluring aura, beckoning, unguarded, almost promising to relinquish herself to any skilled hand— or any threatening firearm.

The portable metal steps glistened invitingly with dew. *How stupid, these Americans, to leave the plane ready for boarding, free for the taking by one such as myself and my devoted soldiers of God,* Mohammed thought. *You could have at least tied a ribbon on our gift, you Western dogs. How foolish your trust! How blind your faith!*

The five terrorists crept ever closer, silently, unseen shadows in the dark chill of the desolate airfield. Frightened, but determined, they scaled the slick metal stairway. Mohammed preceded his fundamentalist brothers and was the first to feel the satisfying give and clunk of the door handle. As if by reflex, he jerked his head up and scanned for security guards. There were none. It had been so easy, so incredibly, exhilaratingly easy. Not one voice was raised, not one bullet was fired. The joy of the break-in's simplicity gushed forth in Mohammed's throat in short gasps interspersed with praises to Allah. It was kismet, divine fate, that had provided this precious prize. Before entering the dark plane, Mohammed dropped to his knees in submission to the very generous and loving Allah.

The five nervously fumbled and groped in the total darkness of the interior of the aircraft. A startling, deafening thud suddenly swallowed the silence, embracing the intruders in a nauseating web of infrasound. Blinding lights flashed on; all was illuminated more brightly than any had ever experienced. Visually stunned, shielding their eyes, growing increasingly terrified, the unprepared men clutched at each other, scrambling behind each other as very small children do behind their mothers at the dentist.

"Allah, save us! This is not an American plane!" Mohammed cried out into the brilliant vastness of the golden circular space. His words, his very voice, deflected off the strange auric metal, repeating back to him in distorted emulation and colored flashes. His brothers in the Holy Quest stood frozen in disbelief, slack-jawed, weapons loosely held at their sides.

"Who is this here?" Mohammed shrieked, huffing. "We demand,

who turns the lights?" Absolute menacing silence. Unshaven faces glanced into other unshaven faces, searching for an explanation, a truth, a prayer.

"Mohammed, this cannot be a plane!" Khaled sputtered. "It—it has more inside than outside!"

A thundering boom escaped from an unknown place into the round room, setting up vibrations through the floor and up into the curved walls. Seized by an unspeakable terror, the five intruders panicked, grasping each other, looking to Mohammed for an explanation, a truth, a prayer.

Assad raised his machine gun and fired randomly at the concave walls. Bullets sprayed haphazardly, zipping from wall to opposite wall, none penetrating, some returning near to their point of origin, passing close by Mohammed.

"Fool! You wish to send me to my God this day?" Mohammed reprimanded, teeth clenched, flashing furious eyes at his over-zealous cohort.

An air-splitting squeal sheared through the atmosphere of the circular room, seeming to come from everywhere at once. "Your weapons are dangerous to your well-being. Do not fire them, you may injure yourselves," a huge, calm voice instructed.

"American dog! What have you done? This is not your decision! Come before us and pray you live!" Mohammed jerked his gun and rammed the stock into his armpit, aiming at nothing.

"You are in error, human. You chose to be here by your own devious designs. And so you shall stay. It is we who now make the decisions.

"You are an interesting subspecies. Near-Eastern, yes?" the voice responded in even, undistressed tones.

"We take this plane! It is the will of Allah! Show yourself now!" Mohammed raised his weapon, crouched and turned slowly on his heel, ready for the entrance of his unseen prisoner. The others cautiously spread out and cowered against the wall, eyes frozen and protruding, staring into the golden emptiness.

Minutes passed, hearts pounded, legs quivered and sweat trickled as the group awaited the emergence of their captive from unseen corridors.

A far wall shimmered and sparkled as the warped air surrendered to the slow materialization of a shapeless presence. It weaved unsteadily—clear, iridescent, colorful vacuoles distorting, growing, shrinking within eddies of swirling, impossibly contained fluid. The entity stared—eyeless; listened—earless; gestured—armless, as a voice asserted its intentions. "I assume you all are the males of your species. How unfortunate you have not brought us females. This will retard our breeding program and resultant commerce in trading your kind."

"You speak nonsense!" Mohammed proclaimed, too angry and intent on completing his holy mission to notice he was not speaking with anything remotely human. "You are our prisoner!" He shuffled sideways along the curved wall, still aiming at the quivering gelatinous mass before him. "We take this...this aircraft! It is ours!"

"Psst. Psst, Mohammed." Khaled removed his cap submissively and whispered to his illustrious leader, "How we take this...aircraft? I see no cockpit, exalted one."

"Shut up, stupid! First hostages—then the cockpit!" Mohammed said in a suppressed growl. Straightening himself as if trying to appear taller, more commanding, he yelled out, "Where are the others? Your crew...tell them to come. We will kill you if you do not cooperate with us!"

The being weaved and bobbed briefly, changing from a soft clear jade green to a bilious yellow shade. "Human—you are in error. It is you who are our captives," it replied.

"Lying American dog!" Tensing and jutting his stubbly jaw, Mohammed stomped up to the creature and watched the tip of his gun sink into the trembling amber jello. Still blinded by his fanatic idealism, refusing to acknowledge the novelty of his situation, he pulled the trigger.

A bullet ripped through and beyond the creature, ricocheting off the wall behind, and zipped back to sink effortlessly into Assad's petrified heart, dropping him like a Persian rug.

Gripped suddenly by the immediacy of his situation, Mohammed jerked backwards, stumbling over his own feet and falling heavily upon the lifeless body of his Muslim brother. Scrambling to his feet, shaking, alternately glancing at the being then down at Assad, Mohammed again bellowed his demands. "We are still four—you have no chance against us! Take this craft away from here!"

"We will be departing in forty-five Earth minutes. Until then, relinquish your weapons and accept your fate. You will be placed in separate confinement areas to prevent any further self-destructive behavior," the unharmed entity explained.

The infrasound hum of the ship grew louder, buzzing the floor and bending the air inside the craft so violently the atmosphere visibly vibrated like the water inside an electric denture cleaning machine.

Voluntary muscles disabled, but fully conscious, the four terrorists collapsed in nauseated, flaccid heaps.

Mohammed felt a gelatinous pseudopod lock onto his skull and drag him along the slick, buzzing floor up to a curved wall. He could see the other three men being pulled in the same manner, sucked along by eerie electric webs coming out the ends of the pseudopods from three other creatures. Low frequency sound poured from his limbs into his bowels; he drooled uncontrollably. He wanted to scream or pray. No sounds would come from his throat.

The captives stomped and screamed at each other from their invisible cubicles, failing to breach the invisible walls between them.

"These new pets show healthy interest in their new surroundings," a trembling being said in the collective voice.

Mohammed spat brown alien gruel at the growing gathering of bobbing, quivering onlookers, and watched it splatter on the unseen barrier before him, streaking the air like a suspended underwear stripe.

"And they seem to enjoy playing with their sustenance as well," another entity observed.

A taller creature flushed in a delicate shade of lavender. "It's so gratifying to see them adjust to captivity so readily. They will make a fine display back on Epsilon Eridani four."

"Hey—fucking mucus bags!" Mohammed protested. "You cannot keep us here!"

"Observe the delightful, colorful colloquialisms which this particular subspecies exhibits. Much more stimulating than the others we've been secretly abducting over the years," a subordinate creature mused.

Directing the voice to Mohammed, the elder said, "Our collection will be enriched by your presence. You will be well cared for, wanting for nothing. Why should you protest this?"

"You cannot just take us like this!" Mohammed cried, his voice higher and more desperate now.

"Of course we can. All of the Universe and all of the other creatures therein are provided to us by the Great Knowing Force, to do with as we wish. The Writings of The Illumination tells us so. Our destiny has been mapped out for us and is not open for debate."

A long, thoughtful pause.

"Most of your kind also embraces this concept; how can you not understand this...this mirror of yourself?"

\* \* \* \*

Fluorescent ceiling lights flickered to life, muting the brilliance of the blue runway lights flashing outside in the grayness of pre-dawn. The control room filled with personnel rushing to their monitors and telephones. The busy, tense room immediately began to smell of strong coffee brewing.

"Well, there she is," Robinson said, looking out at the strange round craft hovering just inches above the concrete airfield. "Get London and Paris on the phone, will you, Lynn?"

"It's hard to believe that thing actually looked like a 747 just hours ago. The cloaking...it was so convincing," Henry remarked.

Lynn interrupted, "London and Paris report identical incidences, sir."

Robinson sat staring thoughtfully into the swirling patterns of cream in his coffee, the tension building inside him like the nervous gnawing of an insatiable hamster.

The windows of the control tower began to shudder delicately. The entire control team jolted to attention and watched as the alien craft lifted slowly into the air, the glowing, whirling, sapphire disk beneath it separated by a foot of empty space, seemingly unattached to the craft, but decidedly responsible for the ship's levitation.

You know," Henry said, arms folded confidently across his chest, "if only we could solve all our problems with the same kind of international cooperation we've seen here today."

"International? Intergalactic! It's perfect—an ideal agreement," Robinson gloated, smiling a malicious rubber smile from beneath the gray foliage of an untrimmed mustache. "The real beauty of it is, we can actually say to these bastard terrorists, 'Don't screw with us. We have allies you have only feared in your dreams,' and mean it."

# RESONANCE

*The quantum jump is the tiniest one, the almost unnoticeable one,
the one that says "maybe" a thousand times before it says "no"
or "yes." It's the one that can change the world forever—
without anyone ever knowing what happened.*

Holotube commercials spewed the virtues of education, advertising this university and that. Ads invaded HT, billboards, magazines, knit shirts, sides of every electropod, and even private data bases. The nation was losing its grip on scientific achievement, they said. Minds were being wasted, they said. Every citizen had a responsibility to get educated, to improve the economy and furtherance of mankind with his mind.

The great machinery of politics dined on the banquet of ignorance; dozens of government agencies supported and were supported by dozens of other government agencies in "the war against ignorance." But there was no war. It was a system designed to feed upon itself. An autophagous monster that used desperate, frustrated minds to keep it alive, to justify its existence.

In fact, no one but the rich could afford a college education; there were no more government grants or loans, no more scholarships. The worst reality was that an increase in educated minds would mean a decrease in the droid workforce, and in the near destitute who scrambled to apply for this service or that benefit, ensuring employment of government paper pushers. Education would upset the balance. And they wouldn't need to build prisons anymore.

\* \* \* \*

Jack walked briskly in the twilight. They were bulldozing an entire block to put up yet another prison. He would have work here for another two months, not more. He wondered how long it would be before he would be sharing a government condo with some other hamster. Work had indeed been hard to find in this town, and before long he'd have to move on before he broke another law or was forced to apply for public assistance. The last option would really be the end. He would become a hamster, running its ass off on some circular wire race course going nowhere. Alive and running, making work for all the public servants, charging up the system which supported him. Leaving to another city would be the only alternative for a man such as himself. Preserve dignity, what was left of it. Duck out gracefully, unnoticed if he was lucky. They'd offered him a substantial government grant for being a Native American, but he had refused to be the oil that greased the gears of the system. At least building prisons was honest work. Even knowing he would probably someday be an inmate in a facility he himself had part in constructing, would be better than validating the system.

Over 87% of the country's population was in prison. Oh, that's not what they called them, but's that's what they were: Controlled Living Facilities, designed to aid the citizen in repaying his debt to society and avoid any further breaches of the law. Outside it was almost impossible to avoid breaking some kind of law daily, there were so many new ones put on the books each day, and many contradicted older laws. Eventually the points added up, and when you accumulated the magic number, you were arrested right in the middle of your grocery shopping, refueling your electropod, or buying some nasty sex toy to spruce up your marriage. The information was all stored on your debit card—every last infraction. It was impossible to keep track of the points in your head, and it was hard to tell how much each violation was worth unless you studied law constantly. Every law had a certain number of points, and when you reached one-hundred twenty-eight, BINGO! your ass was had. No one was ever prepared when it happened to them. "But officer, I didn't know...it can't be one-hundred twenty-eight yet, I've only been in circulation for three years..." That's what they would say as they were being dragged away by their armpits, pleading and making desperate, irrational excuses. Ignorance of the law is no excuse.

As with all other outsiders, Jack had only a vague idea where he stood in the accumulation of violation points. He just tried to keep out of trouble the best he could. He welded steel, punched a time clock and drove home.

Traffic violations were the hardest to avoid. One night he counted five of them, as the lights on his debit card illuminated the dash from its slot and a tinny electronic voice crackled, "Violation recorded. Debit card updated." Most of the time he never knew what the hell he did—or didn't do—to earn those points.

One particularly frustrating experience entailed the check-out of a library book. The electronic librarian had failed to disable the magnetic tape in the book's spine, and Jack's debit card recorded the crime and chalked up the points. His attempts to rectify the situation were futile. Months passed, points accumulated, and overdue fines were levied. The debit card company insisted it was the library's error; the library asserted it was the debit card company's responsibility to rectify the situation. It went back and forth, on and on, a war of shunting responsibility to the other guy, with Jack in the middle, owing at last count, over $4,101 for somebody else's incompetence.

Jack decided to stop off at The Only Tavern In Town on his way home from work. The electropod hummed to a stop a few feet from the entrance of the tidy building, the foothills behind barely contrasting against the blue of the new paint. Jack removed his debit card from the ignition slot and groaned out of the machine, standing stiffly, trying to diffuse the ache in his muscles before he went in the bar. The audible click of the automatic door lock sounded behind him.

Inside the tavern, the music played softly. It was Jack's favorite bar of any city he had worked in, just because he could hear himself think and talk without having to yell. A very pretty redhead sat with something with an umbrella in it at the far end of the bar. Her hair seemed to glow with a life of its own. Jack felt a horniness prance in his loins as he seated himself. It had been weeks since he had been with a woman, not since Theresa had been arrested in Sears for trying to pay for a chemise in the power tool department. Her points were all counted up, and he wouldn't see her for a long time.

The redhead self-consciously tugged at her blouse and flashed a flattered but shy smile at Jack as he stared at her, forgetting his manners.

"Brandy, Jack?" the bartender asked, knowing Jack's habits from months of seeing his face several times a week.

"You got it—make it a triple, George. These thirty-eight year old muscles could use some unkinking. Who's the redhead? Never seen her in here before."

"Me neither. Nice, eh? She's been here about an hour now—same drink. Every guy here's tried to hit on her. Must have a smart mouth, they all slink away with their tails between their legs," George said, chuckling lightly.

"Is that right? I like a woman who knows what she doesn't want." Jack laughed as he glanced over at the flaming cinnamon vision. He quietly sipped measured amounts of brandy, periodically glancing sideways to catch a glimpse of her. He was warming from both ends now, throat coated with liquor, threads of his ever tightening black Levi's radiating heat down his inner thighs. In a moment he would not be able to stand with any modicum of decency. He continued to sip brandy, lost in his fantasies.

Unexpectedly, the redhead was at his side, staring at his long black hair in wonder. "American Indian—beautiful," she said, smiling warmly as she reached out to stroke the hair flowing down his back.

Jack's esophagus seared as brandy shot through his epiglottis, detouring from its proper route. He strained, trying to see through the shimmer of his watering eyes, fighting to avoid exploding into a choke. Alcohol vapors stung his nasal membranes. He was silent for what seemed to him like several minutes, swallowing repeatedly to clear the brandy from his spasming throat.

"I'm sorry. You surprised me," he said in a husky, weak voice.

"I surprise a lot of people," she said.

*I wonder what she meant by that?* Jack thought. He stared into her grass-green eyes, his vision finally clearing. "Why's that? You a rocket scientist...too?" His voice was clear and velvety as he had intended it to be.

She laughed a vibrant, sparkling laugh. "No, just a physics student at Trussdale University. Kaitlin DuBois. Who might you be?"

He hadn't noticed it before, but she had an accent. She definitely had an Irish accent. "DuBois? Sounds French...but you don't."

"Aye, an enigma. A mystery to be read carefully, deliberately," she said, sensuously talking with her eyebrows.

Jack felt uneasy about her riveting eye contact. This woman was not shy, by any means.

"And what do you call yourself?" she asked as she tipped her glass to her full lips.

"Uh...Jack White Horse. Jack." He motioned to George to bring him another triple, never unlocking his gaze from Kaitlin's green eyes. The devil was in them. This woman was going to take more nerve than he had; the brandy served to fortify his courage.

"What tribe, Jack? I've always been fascinated with Indians. Never had one, though."

Jack froze like a rabbit caught in the headlamps of an electropod. Smiling, but still nervous, he answered, "A mix, I'm afraid. It's impossible to tell since the government gathered all the reservations together. That's all that's in Montana now. One big concentration camp of Native Americans." A familiar sadness washed over him. He grew expressionless and reflective.

"But you're here—with me." She gently touched his right leg.

This lady was bold, unbearably, deliciously unnerving. His gaze dropped slowly to scan her voluptuous figure, then returned to her face. She shuddered ever so delicately, as if she had been thoroughly caressed by his wandering hands, instead of only his eyes.

"What do you do here, Horse?"

*Horse? Horse? Yes!* "I usually drink, but tonight things might turn out differently," he answered as he grasped the brandy George had placed in front of him.

Another incredible, alive laugh. "No, I mean, what do you do? Work."

"I build prisons," he said in a monotone as he removed his gaze from Kaitlin and stared into his drink. A cloud of gloom sagged over him as he sat silently, momentarily detached from the excitement of Kaitlin's presence. He gulped more brandy.

"Prisons? You mean Controlled Living Facilities? How long you been doin' that, Horse?"

"Since I left a CLF in '41. I was raised in one. My parents were arrested before I was born. At least the kids start out with a clean slate at eighteen. Twenty years. Twenty years welding girders to imprison somebody else's would-be parents. My mom died in there before she could even earn her way out."

"Why you keep callin' 'em prisons, Horse? They're just places to keep people who've violated the law. Same as here, 'cept they gotta earn their way out again to be more productive citizens. I wouldn't mind bein' in there, if it came to that."

All of a sudden she seemed very stupid, very unaware. That depressed Jack. He had hoped this lady would have enough...God knows she had more than enough of everything else. He impulsively ordered another brandy.

"Hope you plan to stay awhile, Jack. You'll never get into your electropod with all that alcohol in your blood," George said.

"You let me worry about my blood." Jack felt his face tighten and jaws clench as he looked back at Kaitlin. She was beautiful, educated, very sexy, and...brainwashed. Like all the rest. Obviously from a rich family, pampered, sheltered. Little privileged college girl.

"Horse, let's talk some more, at your place."

"You got a vehicle? I won't be able to drive for a while."

"No—I was dropped off by a friend. I was hoping I could get a ride home."

She was obviously planning on getting picked up. Interesting hobby, he thought. She had turned everyone down, George had said. Then she singled him out. Jack's mind was becoming a bit confused and slow as he pondered the enigma beside him. He would do whatever she wanted, he knew it. He could do nothing else, he had to have her.

"Horse, let's get a booth. Talk to me, darlin'." She grabbed his hand and pulled him off the barstool. He followed and flopped down on the cushioned seat, a shit-eating grin overcoming his usually expressionless face. A bright place in the darkness of the system, he thought as he looked at the beautiful Kaitlin seated across from him. A wild, devil-like thing. And her laughter. It was like cold vanilla ice cream in his face after pulling up from a mudhole. Many months had passed since he had shared happiness with another being in this godforsaken city. Horse. She liked to call him Horse. Visions of erotic rides galloped through his slightly inebriated brain.

"Tell me about the CLF. I'd like to be prepared," she said, resting her chin in her hand, elbow propped on the table.

"You wanted by the authorities or something? It's O.K., I'd be the last to blow the whistle on you."

"No, no. Not yet. But you know, we all have to go there eventually. It's good for society that we all do our time in a Controlled Living Facility. Isn't that what they say?"

"Yeah. That's what they say." Jack's face again tensed up into seriousness. "It's like the big cities used to be back in the eighties or early nineties. Rows of identical living quarters covering block after block. Malls, office complexes, some small parks. It's all enclosed now, and nobody can leave till they've earned enough work credits to buy their way out. People stay anywhere from a few months to a lifetime, depending on the grade of work they can put out. Different jobs earn different credits. Any kids born there stay until they're eighteen. They don't know anything but the CLF, so I guess it doesn't bother them. Most of them.

"It always bothered me, especially after hearing stories of my ancestors who roamed the plains of this country, living free out in the open, victims not to each other, but to the highest authority of all— Mother Nature. She was much kinder. She didn't beat at you all the time, just every once in a while to keep you on your toes. There was always hope for better things, if you worked hard enough. Not like in there or...here. Anyway, those are the stories my parents told. I couldn't wait to get out." Jack was silent for two minutes, then sat up straight in his seat to stare Kaitlin in the eyes. "When you get out, you sure as hell don't have an easy time of it. Either you go on public assistance, or you become a droid worker. Some deliberately break more laws to get back in, it's all they can understand, it's all they know. The lucky ones, like me, acquire skills and build more prisons for the unlucky ones."

"You make it sound so bad. The State takes care of you, what's so bad about that?"

"No freedom, lady! No hope of things getting better! You know what I'm talking about? I'll bet not. You protected college elite don't know what it's like for the rest of us. You're only three percent of the population, and you have no concept of what it's like to always be looking over your shoulder for the authorities to pick you up when you're up to one-hundred twenty-eight. You're so rich, you can hire someone to pick your nose for you. You can buy the violation points back!" Jack's voice was loud and resonating. Several customers had stopped their conversation and were staring at him. He slumped back into his seat and quietly swirled his brandy.

"How many times have your relatives or friends bought your points back?" He was whispering this time. He didn't want to insult Kaitlin too much, it would ruin everything.

"Two times," she said meekly.

"Let me tell you something sweetheart. Once you're out of college, you'll be just as vulnerable as I am, unless you're slated for employment within the University. You've racked up two cycles already. How'd you do that? You ever ask yourself that? Did you know you were breaking the law, did it ever occur to you that maybe someday you're going to have to watch your step?" He waited for an answer that never came.

"No, I guess not. You bought all their bullshit, you gave them permission to shove it down your throat," he said. Jack saw Kaitlin's eyes fill with tears in the subdued lighting of the tavern. He had her thinking now.

"In the CLF, no one has any freedoms, personal choices, rights or privacy. You work your ass off at any job you're qualified for. You go home when they say you can go home. You live where they say you can live, shop where they say you can shop. Your electropod is refueled once a month. You don't even have any choice of what you eat, it's all shipped to your quarters. And the Recycling Act, that's a joke. Everyone has a separate room in their house to sort and store the mountains of steel cans, plastic containers, and paper trash the food industry has refused to stop packaging your groceries in. And to top it all off, you have to take it to the recyclers clear across town. No more trash pick-up. They cut your power and water at ten o'clock every night. Tough shit if you want to keep odd hours, watch the holotube or even drink any water after that time. You learn to save water in containers, to sneak things, to stay out of the house at lock-up time so you can camp out in your own back yard. You steal little pieces of freedom. You grab little chunks of rebellion and save them. You're locked in, Kaitlin! Doing everything everybody else does at the same time everybody else does it. There are no taverns, no theaters, no places where too many people could gather in too big a crowd to become a problem for them. Every shit you take is regulated and timed down to the last turd.

"There is no crime. You have to have spirit to commit a crime. You're not really there. When anyone looks at you, they don't see you. There's nobody there to validate you; it's not allowed." Jack watched as Kaitlin squirmed on the leather seat. He had reached some place in her. She was naive, Jack decided, but not stupid, not uncaring. He could teach her. He could teach her how to look around her. He could teach her how lucky she was that she wasn't him.

Kaitlin reached across the table and grasped his left hand, squeezing it almost angrily.

\* \* \* \*

Outside, Kaitlin stood patiently at Jack's side as he eased the debit card into the electropod door slot. Instantly, it was regurgitated, flipping onto the pavement, red lights flashing around the edges. "No damn good. It's getting too high of an alcohol reading from the sweat in my hands. I can't get in the fucking thing yet." Jack's renewed lust was gradually being replaced by anger and frustration again.

"Let's walk," Kaitlin said as she hooked her arm around Jack's.

They ambled onto a freshly watered lawn across the street from The Only Tavern In Town. As they approached a cluster of trees, Kaitlin turned to Jack and hugged him to her, pressing her hips hard against his. Jack eagerly reciprocated and they slumped together in an embrace on the grass.

Their rhythmic motions were rudely interrupted by a distant electronic voice coming from beneath a pile of their clothes, "Violation recorded. Debit card updated."

Jack lurched up. "Who's was that? Yours or mine?" he gasped. Pushing himself to his bare feet, he staggered to the pile of clothes and snatched away a layer. He looked down and saw his own card flashing red, peeking from the inside of his wallet. Next to it, Kaitlin's purse lay dark and silent.

"Goddammit! What the fuck have I done now?" he ranted. Panicked, he furiously began putting on clothes, and caught himself blindly ripping his legs through Kaitlin's panties. "Shit!" He whipped his head around like a trapped coyote, eyes darting in the darkness, waiting for security to scream up and drag him away. It was this way every time. Every time the card went off, he feared for his remaining freedom. Had he reached the magic number yet, was this it? Was it time for him to be taken back to the Controlled Living Facility?

Kaitlin stepped beside him and dressed in the remaining clothes, then grabbed her purse—her silent, dark purse.

Dammit! "Kaitlin, yours didn't go off?" he interrogated.

"No, why should it?" she asked stupidly.

"Screwing in the park used to be a misdemeanor. Your card isn't activated, but it was beside mine..." He stopped speaking abruptly. "Kaitlin, how the fuck old are you?" He cringed in fear of the answer.

"Twenty-four. Why?"

"God! God! God!" Jack stomped around furiously in the grass, looking for all intents and purposes like he was performing some kind of psychotic rain dance.

"Why didn't you tell me? I have no idea how many points statutory rape is! This could be the one, Kaitlin." He stood and huffed, hanging his head. "We gotta get outta here." Jack ripped the now silent debit card from his wallet and hurried to the street. Kaitlin followed, calling after him. He slammed the debit card down on the pavement and smashed a black boot heel into it, fracturing it into several pieces.

No! Jack stop!" Kaitlin shrieked his proper name, watching in astonishment as Jack danced and ground the pieces of his only link to society into the pavement. In a few seconds and several stomps, he had destroyed his hard-earned droid worker status, forfeited his bank account, surrendered his car, his house, his entire life for a few violently victorious moments over the electronic thing that made his life worthwhile on the outside. Jack looked up in his exhausted calm and saw Kaitlin standing there, mouth agape, tears glistening on her face in the light from the tavern signs behind him.

"Jack, how could you do it? You'll get put in CLF for sure now. Even I know it's a crime to destroy or lose a debit card."

"They'll never know," he said calmly. Something untamed and hungry reared up inside him and spread to every pulsing inch of his muscles. He could breathe as never before, feel the blood pumping through his arteries as never before. The sensations were vaguely familiar, yet somehow not. "I'm not reporting it," he affirmed.

"What do you mean? You can't get along without a debit card. They'll find out. They'll catch you," Kaitlin sobbed.

"No they won't. I'm not doing this anymore. They can't have me, I don't belong to them. I'm not playing this goddamn psycho game anymore." He dropped his head again, waiting for an ancient, unknown something to take control of him.

Jack took increasingly deep breaths and clenched his fists. "Sweetheart, it's not worth it." He turned his head and glared into the darkness at mountains he couldn't see. With a great thrust of his thigh muscles, Jack sprang into the air, screaming insanely, long black hair whipping around his shoulders as he dashed wild and determined into the night.

He ran with everything he had, scenery blurring by him in the diminishing light from the tavern. His eyes stabbed into the night. He could make out little bushes and rocks. He ran until he couldn't feel his legs anymore, until the uneven ground disappeared from beneath him. He listened to his heartbeat pounding in his ears, his rhythmic breathing explode from him as he ran deer-like into the brush, towards the mountains. He ripped at his shirt and tore it from his chest, spraying buttons as he ran. His ancestors visited his throbbing brain, showing him the way, calling him, pulling at him as he charged through the trees and bushes. He could see clearly the beautiful plains, the clear blue streams, soaring eagles and a family of wildlife. He was going home. Yes. The gates are open. Yes! With a final burst of raw energy, Jack White Horse made a quantum leap to where his soul had lived forever.

# A CONFESSION

I'm so depressed. I thought I could deal with this, but it doesn't look like that now. You see, I'm dependent on this substance. My whole life is controlled by it; it has infiltrated every aspect of my existence. I know I can't go very long without it, even though I have never really tried. Actually, I feel sick if I try, even for a short period. I'm driven to have it. I just *have* to have it all the time, even though I have read that it is probably slowly killing me. I know it causes damage to just about every cell in my body, but I just can't seem to function without it. Thank goodness it doesn't cost much, or I wouldn't be able to afford it. I guess I should feel ashamed about this dependence, but I don't. Everyone tells me dependencies are dangerous, and that they are a sign of mental or physical illness. I guess I am really sick. I really don't want to give it up...'cuz hell, how can I get along without oxygen?

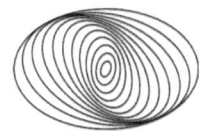

# BAD FEELINGS

Bad feelings are kind of like the laundry. Once a load has been eliminated, you accumulate one piece at time until you have another load. There really is no point at which the basket is ever completely empty.

If you let it go too long, it begins to have a peculiarly recognizable odor. It grows into an ominous mound, finally cascading out into passage ways. It obstructs access to the good stuff a person accumulates through hours of hard work and tedious planning. Finally, this "laundry" has taken over and it has a life of its own—almost wondering at YOU—you who created it and allowed it to flourish out of your inattention and procrastination.

It's time to do the wash.

# A CHILD CONTEMPLATES DEATH

I sat there sickened, saddened by the orange slices. They had tiny veins running through them. They just lay there, dead and bleeding on my plate. They were once alive, hanging from their mother in the sunshine. Now they were dead on my breakfast plate—butchered and bleeding from their tiny veins. Nothing should have to die for me. I couldn't eat them. I pushed the plate away and walked to school empty, sickened and sad for the dead oranges.

That evening, I was so hungry I ate *two* hamburgers at dinner.

## SNOYHCAT

I have so much to say, but no words with which to say it. Success—time for reconversion. To my mind, this has not really unsettled me as much as I had feared; though time runs backwards, my own perceptions refuse to acknowledge anything really unusual in the duration of my trip; time seemed to pass at a normal speed, though I know it could not have. To the outside observer team, my ship and myself have simply disappeared—long ago—having already been recorded as a tachyon shower almost an hour earlier.

My mind is running forward, it seems, while everything around me, including my own body, is speeding in reverse through space-time, taking me to the place where I have already arrived. I know I will be driven to press the respective buttons. The console lights flicker off then back on in bizarre, unpredictable patterns. I must have said that later, or is it earlier? I hear my own voice say, "God, how fucking uninteresting. Not what I expected." Absolute nothingness. Just a boring flat two-dimensional gray. I look out the porthole and see...gray. A wave of nausea envelopes me.

I flip the activation/conversion switch. Help me. "One," oh God. "Two," I wish I knew how to pray. "Three," Even a rat shouldn't have to endure this. "Four," At least if I piss my pants, they'll be clean when I get back. "Five," I wonder if my palms will un-sweat? "Six," Take it easy Andy. "Seven," No turning back now. "Eight," I can hardly breathe I'm so rattled. "Nine," Halfway there. "Ten."

The voice counts down reassuringly, steadily.

"Yeah, let's go for it."

*Ready for countdown, Andrew?* I ask myself.

The duality of determinism and chaos frightens me. The ominous responsibility sickens me. I suddenly feel overwhelmed by the realization that I am responsible for everything that happens in this universe—according to my perceptions and the perceptions of all the observers. My choices will determine what happens. Mind boggling. I would not have traveled through time, for I would not have arrived almost an hour from now, if I didn't flip the switch. The instructors told me it wouldn't make any difference—that in this universe, I would have to flip it. As the time for departure neared, my mind toyed with the possible effects of not flipping the switch for conversion.

Needless to say, controlled panic has mutated into alert anticipation. I will choose no other course of action—the quantum wave function has already been popped. In an hour I will flip the toggle switch on the console; I have already arrived. A team member reported a huge surge of tachyons detected when I was barely leaving.

In effect, I must arrive fifteen degrees longitude west of where I left, in an infinitesimally tighter universe than the one I am positioned in now. All factors seem to be in order, calculated to place me in the there and then that existed before I left on my eerie backwards journey through space-time at superluminal speeds. The the expansion of the universe, the position of Earth on an outer arm of the Milky Way, Earth's position in its journey around the sun, as well as the rotation of the Earth, have been taken into account. Everything has been worked out mathematically to the twelfth decimal place. I check the log one last time. The calculations for replacing me to the proper space-time must be exact—or I have will died.

The only evidence the team had that something actually happened will be the detection of a great surge of tachyons bouncing through an electrical field about an hour before I am converted. In an instant this ship and everything in it will cease to exist—just for a split second— to outside observers as I scream through space-time, composed of all tachyons, unable to travel *but* at superluminal speeds. Although I can't see it above me, a matter conversion chamber rests in its long probe, aiming at the ship, ready to spray an intense field around me, through me, and through this fiberglass encasement they call a ship. Through the porthole of the ship I study the walls of the mega-cyclotron—a giant version of the old particle accelerators.

There's a knot in my guts as I try to ponder, try to imagine how it will be. I can feel my helmet barely grazing the ceiling of this egg-shaped capsule. The quarters are suffocatingly cramped. I can't believe I am actually going to go through with this.

The human mind probably wouldn't be able to deal with too many cause-effect violations all at once. The trip would last less than an hour, they assured us. My instructors explained we wouldn't be superluminal long enough to have to deal with very much of our own biology. That one remark created a bit of restrained laughter, which lead to other questions regarding bodily functions in reversed time. I had to get sassy in class and ask an instructor what it might be like to see a booger materialize on your finger, and shove it back in your nose. All of that would be rather easy to take, like watching a movie run backwards. The academy spent months training us not to crack mentally when we heard our words before we spoke them, saw the control panel light up before any buttons were pushed, or even observed a supernova implode into a stable star. The experts expected we would see many odd, out-of-sequence events. I suspected it could rip a man's mind apart if he couldn't maintain that "interested observer" attitude; especially the psychological effects of superluminal travel. They know I have a tendency to back out of things once I understand them. They've tried to explain it to me, but I'm just an experimental human who got talked into this crazy thing, (And I guess, not really wanting to know) not really knowing what it was I would be doing.

It will be just a few minutes before this ship is converted to tachyons, with me inside, watching myself do things out of their proper sequence—backwards—arriving safely back in my own space-time before I have left.

It is nearly time for my uncertain journey to begin. A surge of tachyons has been detected very near where my ship waits. I know the last vestiges of confidence I feel won't last for long.

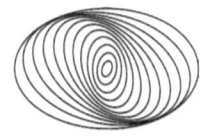

# HOW I SPENT MY SUMMER VACATION

Flat tire.

No choice, gotta get out.

Shit, I'll never live through it. I'll be smeared all over the freeway by some creep hogging his way through an eight-foot space in an eight-and-a-half-foot-wide RV. He'll clip me, unaware, and drag my screaming body thirty feet—my hand still clutching the jack handle—before I fall away, tattered and mangled and unconscious, awaiting the final brutality of tread patterns ironing my meat into the road. By the time the wife and kids miss me, I'll be but a grimy blotch unceremoniously crammed into the concrete grooves of Interstate-5. I'll be just a memory, a deranged collection of unrecognizable but somehow familiar molecules, a gory shadow of my former self.

And I'll still have a flat tire.

Mustering the demented courage of a matador, I hug the stack of orange road cones liberated from an accident scene several miles back, and plop them strategically around the marooned Winnebago. At least my life insurance is up to date, I think as I hurry furiously to change the tire.

Finished. Amongst the living—still.

My stomach retreats cowardly behind my spleen as a huge jacked-up pick-up—you know, the kind that requires stilts to get in it—brushes my pant leg as it lumbers by, crumpling a cone into an unidentifiable fistful of orange polyethylene. A miss is as good as a mile, the wife likes to say. Oh no it isn't; I've never shit my pants just missing that semi five blocks down the road.

Getting back into the ooze of traffic would be about as easy as sewing a button on a poached egg. The kids are screaming and taking out their low blood sugar on each other's heads.

"Ow!" Billy howls. "Stop it! Dad! Cindy's poking me with her anti-nausea chip! Ow! Dad—make her stop!"

"Dammit Cindy! I told you not to pick at the incision—now the whole thing's fallen out and sooner or later you'll be car sick, barfing down your mother's back again.

"Pam, can you get back there and see if you can reinsert it? It goes behind the left ear this time. See if the wires are still intact. Jesus, Jesus, if I have to pay for another neural-medullary rechanneling...."

On top of that, the usual battle over what and where we would be eating, commences. No one could agree as I weaseled the monstrosity of an RV back onto the clogged freeway.

As usual with each approaching month-end, Pam and I had fought viciously for the three days before I finally knuckled under and took the family on their two-week odyssey. I knew if I ever won this one and stubbornly stayed home—"held captive" (as the wife likes to say) by my custom-fitted Cybervision device, can of beer welded to my hand, watching those three-day-long football games—she would murder me in my sleep.

It was hard enough on me beating my brains out in Washington for six weeks straight; having to take the family out on this two-week nightmare of recreational curses was almost unforgivable. I remember before we embarked on this month-end ritualistic torture, how I promised to myself I would take my own life if things got too hairy for me. It would have to be quick but suitably grotesque—gory enough to haunt those self-centered demanding little faces for the rest of their lives. I'd want it to say: "Oh God, look what we made daddy do. How could we be so insensitive?"

"God, how could this happen? *How* did it happen?" I mutter to myself.

"John, why don't you just lighten up and enjoy your time with your family? We don't see you for six weeks at a time, and when we finally all get together all you do is bitch, bitch, bitch," Pam snaps.

Damn. I didn't plan on her hearing my remark. Here we go again. This argument has been going on for eight years that I can remember—interrupted by intermissions of eating and sleeping.

"You know it's all crap. I've been telling you this for years. It's just another brilliant Government scheme brewed up to revive the floundering recreation industry. Can't you see how miserable we all are? We're killing ourselves with these vacations!"

"Six-week work-months with two-week month-ends are keeping the American family together. That's why it was written into law in 2028. You're such a pessimist," Pam said.

Damn the ostriches. She had been thoroughly sucked in, just like those assholes in Washington who were obliged to ignore the flip-side of this "hurry up and recreate" mentality.

It isn't the first time I've been accused of having a bad attitude. My visions of doom are not only ruining my marriage, they have prompted my superiors to shuttle me off into an obscure corner of the White House so I won't bother anyone with my predictions of disaster. "Senator Thompson's one tree short of a hammock," I'd hear them whisper.

I have no doubt the wife feels the same way about now.

"Here we all are, canned in an RV, monstrous suitcases packed to the ceiling, crawling for two weeks through ten-mile-an-hour traffic, praying we find a fast food line with a wait less than an hour. Tell me what the hell's to be optimistic about!"

"For one thing, we have a nice space at the campsite. And the kids just love looking through the telescope at night. The view is so much clearer than back home."

"Jesus, Pam. I had to reserve that space three years in advance! The place is absolutely packed. People scream at each other all the time. Hell, the tension's so high strokes are routinely treated by first aid officers! How is this good?" I'm losing the control I promised to myself I would maintain. "As for skygazing, who wants to look at garbage in geosynchronous orbit?"

"If the telescope isn't too powerful, it's almost beautiful."

It was hopeless. Pam had lost all of her discrimination as well as her good sense. "I fail to find esthetic appeal or entertainment value in man's excesses and flagrant waste. I'd rather be at home watching the game."

"How do you find plugging into Cybervision and going into a touchdown fugue entertaining? Since they began playing with relay teams and the games last for three or more days at a time, you disappear. You emerge only to gather munchies and beer so you can go under for the next game.

"I'm worried you could become addicted to Snooze Ender. You take twice the normal dosage so you'll never miss a second of action."

She pauses briefly, gulping a labored breath, then resumes her ranting. "The only time you even spend time with the kids is when they lead you back and forth to the toilet. You won't even take off those damn goggles for that. What value could all of this possibly have? Do you want to escape from me, from your family? Is that it?"

Pam's voice betrays her. She's about to turn on the waterworks—again. I should never have told her how much I hate it when she cries. My guts ball up, only partly from hunger.

"Look, Daddy! An accident!" Cindy shrieks.

"Jesus, there goes another family's nest egg. At this speed accidents disfigure rather than kill. I can just hear the plastic surgeons rubbing their hands together now. What happened to the good old days when people died gloriously with a steering wheel imbedded in their lungs? Or the emergency teams would have to pry your face out of a dashboard, and it would come up looking like the grill off a '47 Buick?

Sure as hell would solve the over-population problem if people died in cars like God intended."

"John, you're so morbid. Please don't talk like that in front of the kids."

"Daddy, I'm hungry!" Billy complains.

"When we get by this wreck, it'll be easier to find a food outlet with a short line. Have you decided what you want?" I ask futilely.

"Daddy, let's go to Taco Nation," Cindy cheers.

Billy wraps his sweater around her head, whining, "We went to Taco Nation two days ago! Can't we go to Burger Breeze this time?"

Pam glances back at Billy with her You-should-be-flogged look, turning a subtle shade of chartreuse. She has nearly become a vegetarian since Burger Breeze and some supermarkets have installed slaughter houses right behind their businesses, speeding up the moo to mouth production time for an ever increasing, ever impatient populace.

"Cluck-in-a-Bucket would be a nice change," I suggest. Even Pam will concede to this. She says the chickens are drugged before they are killed, and their deaths aren't audible from the ordering area. Steers, on the other hand, always bellow that one last forlorn protest which tends to take the edge off even the heartiest of appetites.

The line isn't as long as we had feared—only fifty minutes. I lean out of the window and punch the picture keys on the order platform of the tollbooth-sized enclosure, and listen in anticipation as little servo-motors retrieve our food from the underground robot-controlled food preparation lab. The food has never been touched by human hands; the days of the illiterate, zit-eroded, nose-picking food handler are long gone—thank God.

Of course, Billy didn't want chicken, but he ate it anyway. Everyone fed, we start our fourteen mile, two-hour drive to that cartoon character hell: Disneyland.

"I hope they have enough Benzo-Ped vendors there this time," Pam says wistfully.

I hope they sell loaded guns, I think darkly. I wasn't sure I could ever be ready for what awaits us inside those gates. I momentarily wish that I would just drop dead from some fortuitous stroke, but with my luck I wouldn't be going to paradise as my priest had assured me I would; I'd be sentenced to stand in some interminable line at an amusement park for all eternity.

I take a deep breath and prime my squeakiest voice. "Welcome to Miseryland! This is Morose Mouse. Minnie died today. We'll be having the funeral just as soon as we scrape her marginally identifiable body from beneath one of the spinning teacups. Looks like the makings for a real down-home anniversary wake. Should boost our profits better than any—"

"Shut the fuck up, John! You promised me you wouldn't do this," Pam howls.

"Sorry. Just trying to make the four mile walk to the entrance less of a drag."

We arrive early enough to catch a glimpse of someone in a cute blond bear suit slip into the stockyards behind a burger restaurant, attempting to conceal some long device, on his way to prepare for the forthcoming supper crowd. The idea of Winnie the Pooh shoving an electric prod up a cow's ass sends cold chills through my bowels. But that's the way it is now, and no one ever gives it a second thought. The kids have grown especially indifferent to it.

We purchase our Benzo-Ped sandals and near the last hour and a half of our three-and-a-half-hour wait in line for Space Mountain. Pam's feet and legs, as well as my own, are pleasantly numbed clear to the waist, but Cindy is acting a bit strange, unable to control her arms or her tongue. Billy just seems spaced-out, staring out blankly into the kelp-bed of distressed, shuffling humanity. He'll be fine by the time it's our turn, but Cindy is another matter.

"Don't you think we ought to take her to a first-aid station, John?"

"I'm not getting out of this goddamn line for anybody! The devil himself will have to set me on fire! She's got a little too much drug in her system, that's all. Just take off her sandals. She'll snap out of it."

And she did. And we got our ride—our three-minute ride.

Dinner at Donald's Salad Pond. The entire Crass Family tries to move in ahead of us in line, mumbling something about there being too goddamn many people out on vacation. I reply with something like, "People who shit in glass toilets shouldn't eat stones," before I am able to close up the gap ahead of us and thwart their audacious advance.

Buy more Benzo-Peds; stand in line for three more hours. Scream and laugh. I'm glad this day is nearly over—I may not kill myself after all. I can't wait to get out on that freeway for a leisurely crawl back to San Diego, police hovercrafts harassing us all the way. Another Fuckation over and done with.

Both kids drink their Coma-In-A-Drum and will be asleep for three days—just long enough for me to recover and charge back to Washington to put in another grueling six weeks. It'll be dawn before we get home—what's left of it.

Robotic highway maintenance crews clear the last of a grove of pollution-killed redwoods as a rusty red sun groans up through the smog-choked dawn horizon. Two more exits and we'll be pulling into our driveway. After all these years, I still have nervous currents fleeting through my viscera each time we come back from month-end vacations.

Making the final turn, I scan the houses. There's one. And another. Only two this time; that must be some kind of low record. A burglary rarely leaves a house in decent shape; inevitably it'll have to be renovated. Oh God, please don't let my house be one of the statistics. Those bastards couldn't have broken the security system this time. The security company assured me it would take many months and an entire gang of thieves to break all the codes. They'd better be as sure as I am paranoid.

Creaking the RV into the driveway, the breath I am holding gushes forth, startling Pam from her light doze.

"Everything's OK this time," I say.

Pam stretches and looks around. "Yeah, for us—but look. The Bartons got it."

"Jesus, they'll be banging on our door the minute we get in. Don't summon the cybermaid to collect the kids, we'll carry them in ourselves. Be quiet, we don't want to alert the Bartons."

"Too late, here comes Tom. He's not navigating too well either."

Tom Barton staggers up to the driver's side of the RV, almost snagging the ass of his pants on a rosebush. "You lucky bastards. They missed your place three month-ends in a row. We got hit bad. Took everything, tore out the walls, ripped up the carpet to get the floorboards up. Lucky they didn't go through the ceiling, that's where Cecilia keeps her silver service—in the crawl space."

"Tell Cecilia you can all stay at our place until you get your house back together," Pam said, leaning over me, her slender neck straining as she generously offers our neighbors refuge in a home I have only two days left to appreciate. If I had a rope....

"You got insurance, though. Right? It shouldn't be too long before your house is ready." At last, a little optimism surfaces. I try to be concerned. I am—for me.

"No...let the payments lag. I ain't got work yet. Nobody hires on month-ends anyhow. But, I'll be lookin' next work-month," Tom slurs as his eyeballs switch sockets and he steadies himself by clutching the door handle.

"That's only three days from now, man. How long you been stoned?" My false hope erodes to dread.

"The whole month-end. I'll be sober enough to get work. Don't you worry."

"Listen here, Mr. Herbalife. With these long month-ends, it isn't the same as before when we had only two-day weekends to get loaded, then straighten up before Monday."

"It don't make me no never mind anyhow. Can't figure to fill out the employment application," Tom sighs.

I glare over at Pam, wanting to show my gratitude for her samaritanism with a chokehold.

Resigning myself to the situation, we pile out of the van, unconscious kids in arms, stoned neighbor and family trailing.

After several minutes, all thirty codes are cleared by the security system, and the front door sweeps open—and stops halfway. A mountain of FAX paper cascades through the opening. It looks like the whole box of paper—all five thousand feet—has been blown this time. What a bitch when standard mail delivery is suspended. It'll take weeks to sift through it to find the important stuff amid all the junk-mail ads like, Dick's Odor Control Toilet Seats and A1 Portable Circadian Rhythm Adjustment Devices and Quiet Rampage Cat Food: one packet feeds twelve.

I smile evilly to myself as I envision Pam dealing with her house guests on her own. I'll be gone in two days; work will be a merciful relief from vacations.

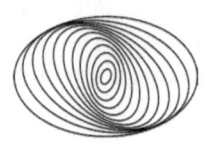

# THE NOBLEST PROFESSION

It was time to get up. His mind told him that, but his body had not been prepared, and it was still dark. It was absolutely as dark as a black hole. The wrist unit should not have awakened him until dawn. Nicolus strained his eyes in the darkness, trying to make out the vaguest outlines of the pictures hanging on the wall in his quarters. He could see nothing. It was peculiar to him that his room was so obscure and undefined, and so completely quiet. It was a kind of quiet he had never experienced before. He attempted to roll over; a surge of panic gripped him. He wasn't moving—he couldn't. A feeling like a gush of heavy sand poured into his limbs and trickled to a tingle as all sensations gradually disappeared. He couldn't even feel his body pressing against the bed where he lay. Something was terribly wrong. He was seized by absolute terror—or at least he thought he was. It was a strange, unspeakable kind of terror. It was an isolated mind-terror, unaccompanied by any familiar physical sensations whatsoever. He felt no fire of adrenaline rushing through his veins, no pounding heartbeat, no frantic breathing or sweating, no sickening gut-twisting visceral response. Nothing. His mind was engulfed in sheer panic, as the horror of his aloneness, his helplessness, his need to be discovered, swallowed him in a vacuum of nothingness. Nicolus tried to cry out— he didn't feel his mouth open; he could make no sound. He couldn't hear anything except his own increasingly loud voice calling out—screaming inside his head. He kept screaming until his entire consciousness was saturated with the irrational belief that if Aura, if Macedonia—if anybody stood close enough to him, they could hear the sounds coming from his head. Someone had to hear him. It was deafening.

\* \* \* \* \* \*

Aura slowly and quietly slipped into Nicolus' room. She smiled a silly, smitten smile to herself as she studied his beautiful, peaceful sleeping face. He seemed so detached from the grueling demands of his work with the neural-computer. It was 9:30 A.M., quite late indeed for Nicolus to still be sleeping. His breathing was slow and deep—the breathing of one blissfully unaware of all outside activity and removed from life's hassles. Aura stepped out of the room to leave him for just a while longer. One should not disturb the needs of a brilliant mind; Nicolus was obviously overworked.

In the main quarters where Aura returned, Macedonia grew

restless. He paced the dome and neurotically leaped from one piece of furniture to the floor, and back onto the furniture. He glared at Aura. Macedonia's insistent eye contact caused a great uneasiness in her. Aura silently wished that she knew what he was thinking.

It was 11:00 A.M. when Aura found herself standing at Nicolus' bed, wondering with increasing concern why he still slept. He had not even changed positions. Nothing had changed; not his breathing rhythm, not his facial expression—nothing. Aura felt an overwhelming fear grow inside her.

As Aura reflected on Nicolus' curious restfulness, Macedonia anxiously trotted into Nicolus' quarters, meowing his battery of questions. He pounced upon Nicolus' bed and methodically paced up and down the length of his still body. Nicolus didn't even so much as flinch when Macedonia absentmindedly planted a paw squarely in his crotch.

Leaning down, Aura gently stroked Nicolus' thick black hair, speaking to him in urgent tones. There was no response. She shook his shoulders, then pinched his arm, then pulled his eyelids back. Growing increasingly distressed, Aura pried open his mouth and rudely shoved her finger down his throat. There was not even a gag reflex. Aura quickly yanked his left arm up, gazing at the wrist unit attached to his arm. Nicolus offered no resistance or even the slightest registration of Aura's manipulations. Seeing that all basic vital signs read normal, Aura deftly removed the wrist unit, and after carefully sealing the radial vein with a wax plug, dashed out of the room to the wall unit.

After interfacing the wrist unit, the computer hesitated for what seemed like several minutes, and finally blinked into full response. The read-out was like something from a cheap horror movie. Aura felt sweat oozing down her sides; her panic waxed as she poured over the data. "Oh, God...no," she wept. "God...no." Her fingers zipped over the keyboard, entering commands and requests, calling up screen after screen of unbelievably impossible data. It was hours before Aura could sift out the pertinent from the incidental. By all indications, Nicolus was in a deep, possibly irreversible coma. So Aura reasoned.

In the midst of all of her scientific objectivism, she was suddenly jolted by the reality of the situation; her best friend, a man she loved, was apparently gone. In intense desperation, Aura began gathering equipment and pharmaceuticals, moving them into Nicolus' quarters.

Aura fervently began connecting electrodes to Nicolus' scalp, working her way through his thick hair with the putty tube. Aura's residual hope faded into grief and resignation as she prompted the electroencephalograph. The waves on the screen were almost all flat. Almost—except for an occasional peculiar spike on the theta line. She watched it, mesmerized by the oddity of its appearance. It was perfectly regular, it had rhythm, and an unchanging amplitude. Every twelve seconds, there it was. "Theta?" Aura spoke aloud, startling herself. "Theta waves just don't show up in the comatose." She knew theta waves indicated active thought, or emotional stress—and they were regular at five to eight cycles per second. They didn't occur in spikes as those now revealed coming from Nicolus' chemically confused brain. Aura's eyes were pulled into the screen as she stared at it. The spikes were so perfectly regular, they just couldn't be a malfunction.

Impulsively, Aura jabbed Nicolus in the ribs as she fixed her eyes on the EEG screen. Nothing changed. He was not awake, nor was he meditating, nor was he sleeping.

A large theta spike played its perfect dance on the green phosphor monitor. Aura mused that it was almost like code. She contemplated the patterns for many minutes, then, urged by uncertainty and desperation, she switched off the EEG, waited five seconds, and turned it back on. This time all waves were flat, confirming Aura's previous suspicion. Aura embraced her abdomen, bent over in her chair and cried her silent, suffering cry. She had lost him.

"Nicolus, I am so sorry. I never could have foreseen anything like this when I" -BLIP- "decided to undertake this" -BLIP- "project...." Aura gaped in astonishment at the screen, almost angry at it for mocking her. But there they were again: those incredibly perfect spikes, playing out on the screen like some kind of musical score! Could some part of his brain still be conscious? The question seemed ludicrous as Aura asked it again and again to herself.

\* \* \* \* \* \*

Aura aimlessly sauntered around the dome as she mentally developed, mixed and measured the proper dosage of stimulant that could possibly bring Nicolus back. Macedonia followed her, meowing his questions incessantly. Four hours had passed since Aura had discovered Nicolus' condition. Then, unexpectedly, the combination of drugs seared like an acid bath into her thoughts. She gathered up her fortitude and returned hurriedly to his quarters where he lay in his tranquil, unknowing state.

Aura drew small portions of several different brain stimulant compounds into the syringe. Knowing she was risking a great deal—namely what was left of Nicolus' life—she proceeded with determination. Cautiously, she prepared Nicolus' right arm for injection, then slid the needle into his distended vein.

Outside, in the main quarters, Macedonia became increasingly agitated. In a spasm of excitement, he tore around the dome and shot into Nicolus' quarters, where the big event was beginning to unfold. Aura watched in amazement as Macedonia zoomed around the small room, barely touching anything but the sides of the walls in his blur of Siamese delirium.

\* \* \* \* \* \*

Nicolus heard a buzzing sound inside his head, like a thousand angry bees trapped in a Mason jar. It grew louder and louder, until it completely masked his own disoriented, turbulent thoughts. He could hear nothing but the maelstrom of horrid buzzing. It seemed to go on forever as his fear returned in full force. Nicolus screamed inside his head; he didn't hear it. Thoughts of death, fear of death, wishes for death, clawed at his buzzing brain. He was certain he would hear the hideous buzzing for eternity. He was powerless to reduce the volume, to over-think it, to shut it off. It was one with him. It was him.

Progressively, Nicolus felt faint tingling sensations in his arm and hands. The tingling radiated to his chest and abdomen and down his legs, growing in vigor. Suddenly, Nicolus realized that he still had a body, that he was not paralyzed, nor quasi-dead. Through the constant buzzing in his head, he salvaged a glimmer of relief and hope. At the same time, an accumulating sense of dread dampened his short-lived confidence: his body no longer tingled, but buzzed,—like the buzz in his head. It was a grotesque, unbearable sensation that compressed and lacerated his very soul. Nicolus screamed inside his head.

Aura lurched back in shock and slammed against the wall as Nicolus' tortured scream flooded the room, discharging off every surface. She saw his contorted face and straining body quiver in a film of fresh sweat. He babbled incoherently, gasping for air, then slumped silently into a guarded relaxation, still holding wads of bedclothes in his clenched fists. Aura stood frozen in disbelief as she stared, watching both the EEG screen and Nicolus. His brain waves had miraculously returned to normal, almost as if he were engaged in casual conversation. He was certainly alive, and probably conscious, but his return from wherever, had not been a pleasant one.

The several seconds of nightmarish struggle and nonsensical

utterances had ceased. His face returned to a peaceful, pleasant appearance; then Nicolus began to sob as his eyes opened to the welcome sight of the ceiling of his quarters. And there to his right, stood Aura, looking down at him like a priest delivering the last rights. "Aura? What happened to me? Did you do this to me?" Nicolus begged as tears streamed down his face and puddled in his ears.

Aura ignored his near accusations, "What happened to you? Where were you?" she asked firmly, grasping his right hand.

Nicolus' speech was shaky and disjointed , but coherent. "I—I don't know. At first I felt like I didn't have a body...like my brain was somehow suspended in this incredibly dark, completely silent anti-gravity chamber. Nothing I could do would convince me that I even had a body; it just didn't exist. I even thought for some time that my body was dead, and it would just take a while for my brain to catch up. I...I couldn't see, hear, feel—NOTHING. I was completely alone, unable to experience anything but my own thoughts. I screamed as loud as I could; I wanted somebody to hear me. Did you hear me? Did you hear me, Aura?"

"I didn't hear you until a minute ago, when I administered the stimulant. You screamed your lungs out, scared the catshit out of Macedonia, and gave me a nosebleed," Aura explained sarcastically.

Nicolus' face took on a puzzled expression. "The buzzing. That Godawful buzzing. Did the stimulant do that? I don't remember ever getting that effect from a stimulant before."

"Here's what I think happened. It appears that your wrist unit malfunctioned; it failed to deliver your usual wake-up stimulant, which allowed your GABA and serotonin levels to climb. You were in a deep coma...your reticular activating system wasn't responding. The stimulant caused a torrential flood of awareness of all internal and external activity. You heard the white noise of life, Dear Nicolus. Most of us never hear it because our brains selectively filter out everything that isn't important, which is damn near everything." Aura took his hand and eased him off the bed.

\* \* \* \* \* \*

"What time is it?" Nicolus asked as he sat gazing through the dark window glass at the huge, cold, red sun consuming the horizon. His hands shook slightly as he sipped from his cup of sweet ethanol.

"It's 6:30 PM Same day, by the way."

"Same day as what? How long was I—'gone'?" Nicolus asked cautiously.

Aura turned to him, shifting in her chair. "Tuesday. I found you at 9:30 in the morning, when I first suspected something was wrong. I assume the wrist unit module was malfunctioning from dawn, your normal wake-up time. I have to finish my analysis before I can really tell what happened to your chemistry balance. The Foundation should be notified of this, you know. Not only did you not logon for your assignment today, but they'll want to know if any of the units are not working properly."

"And my ass is the front lawn. How are we going to explain that our perfect solution to stabilizing human biochemistry through venous-neural interface, a device now being used by thousands all over the globe, is possibly defective and may send the users to the outer reaches of sanity?" Nicolus became troubled with his question as he listened to it leave his mouth. The economical and political implications were beyond his ability to estimate.

"You know," Nicolus reflected, "I feel this overwhelming urge to consult with Rod Serling."

"Who's Rod Serling?" Aura queried.

Nicolus smirked; she should know this, at her age. "He was a rather brilliant philosopher of the mid-20TH century who wrote sophisticated philosophical plays under the guise of science fiction and fantasy. His ideas and observations were so disturbing to some that he never really caught on as a philosopher. Kind of a shame. He'd love what I just went through."

"You mean, like you're experiencing some kind of moral dilemma," Aura said, "and your subconscious robbed you of your body temporarily, so maybe you would snap back with a whole new perspective on life? Some kind of crap like that?" Aura strained to keep from laughing at Nicolus' expense.

"Not exactly, Aura," Nicolus retorted, grimacing. "but, you know how I feel about some of the work we do for the Foundation. I remember an incident when I was working in the Foundation laboratory before we could work out of our domes. There was this woman lab assistant that would try damn near anything. The whole lab used her for every friggin' experiment that needed to be confirmed, no matter how bizarre or insane it seemed, no matter how dismal the projected outcome. It scared me to think just how far they would go to get results.

"She wasn't stupid, just submissive...I guess that's another way of being stupid. Submission to anything other than your own temptations is stupid, and it should never happen unless you give yourself permission. "She almost died twice. The last time, it did kill her. I almost forgot that. I almost forgot all about that. Anybody like that woman would be a valuable asset to scientific research, ethics aside. I wonder how the Foundation ever got along without her...." Nicolus' voice trailed off as his face assumed a serious veneer.

* * * * * *

Nicolus slept a fitful sleep. He was without his wrist unit for the first time in four years, and was completely unaccustomed to his own natural biological cycles. To make matters worse, his chemistry had not resumed its normal patterns (and wouldn't for several weeks), and many hormones and neurotransmitters were askew, adding to his discomfort. He constantly shifted and turned in his bed, thinking of his ordeal, thinking about how awful, yet—somehow, how wonderful it had been. Terror is an all-consuming emotion. Had he not freaked-out, he may have learned something important. No matter how long he talked to Aura, the full impact of his adventure could never be related to her. And, incredibly, she even pretended to know exactly what had happened. Arrogant medical genius bitch, Nicolus thought. Even he, a well-respected neural-computer programmer with an adequate background in neurophysiology, could not fully comprehend the intricacies of the human brain and mind. But, their extraordinary talents and value to the Foundation were the reason Nicolus and Aura had been assigned together. They alone developed the wrist unit module; they alone were answerable to the Foundation for any unexpected complications with the unit. In a familiar, but long forgotten melancholy defeatist attitude, Nicolus agonized over explaining the failure—his failure—to the Foundation luminaries. Ironically, Nicolus thought, the coma and revival would seem like just a bad dream, compared to the consternation and reprimands of the ruling board of the Foundation. They would make more noise than a nude fat man sliding down a Naugahyde fire pole.

He fleetingly considered not telling them, but dismissed this idea as immoral and unethical, not to mention how Aura would react; she was so righteous sometimes. Nicolus suspected she only acted that way to torment him. She delighted in annoying him—just like her damned cat. What a perfect pair. And they were assigned with him; of hundreds of scientists, it had to be him. Even as Nicolus spasmodically slept, his apprehension of the certain confrontation with the Foundation gnawed at his insides for the several hours before dawn.

\* \* \* \* \* \*

At breakfast, Macedonia sat on the floor to Nicolus' right side. Macedonia wasn't interested in his own breakfast. He didn't move, and seemed to be breathing in controlled puffs, as he intently watched Nicolus eat.

"What's the matter with this damned cat? If his eyes were lasers, I'd be Swiss cheese," Nicolus complained.

"He's just concerned, I imagine. You know how sensitive CBT cats are. You should have seen him yesterday when you were coming out of your fog; he was absolutely crazed. He knows I'm concerned; he feels it, so naturally...."

"No, this is different. He's really getting on my nerves. Can't you call him away or something?" Nicolus quickly interrupted, shoving another spoonful of triticale into his tense mouth.

"Geez, Nicolus. A few hours of disturbed sleep, and you think creatures are out to get you. He's just a cat. He isn't on your wavelengths; he's calibrated to me. It's me, Nicolus. Macedonia feels what I feel."

"And just what is that, besides your usual aloof scientific curiosity?" Nicolus snapped. "And tell me, do you feel anything when you institute your faultless medical expertise? Are you ever turned on? Or is it just strictly business as usual?"

Aura cringed visibly as his words bit into her like a monitor lizard. Not saying another word, she jealously scooped up Macedonia in her arms and stomped off to her quarters. The analysis and repair of his wrist unit could not come too soon.

Putting his spoon down and propping his elbows on the table, Nicolus sank his head into his hands, immediately regretting everything he had just said. Sighing deeply in his melancholy way, Nicolus pulled himself up and stood, wondering what he could say to Aura to rectify his childish transgressions. Besides, her medical expertise was the only way he would be able to logon to the Foundation Network, now that the wrist unit wasn't connected and taking constant readings from his blood and neural activity.

Nicolus quietly and humbly approached the closed door to Aura's quarters, boyishly hanging his head and keeping his arms close to his body. He spoke gently and precisely.

"Aura, I'm sorry. I don't know what's the matter with me—maybe the wrist unit is more important to my well being than I thought. Please, will you help me reconnect and logon to the Foundation? I have to tell them what happened—about the malfunction."

A few difficult seconds passed, then Aura opened the door, holding a gloating, purring Macedonia in a motherly embrace. Jesus, cats really do smile, Nicolus thought as he fixed his lowered eyes on the spoiled feline.

"Yeah—O.K. I guess you really are more screwed up than I thought. I mean, your chemistry has gone haywire—not that you are intrinsically screwed...forget it." Aura blundered through her acceptance of his semi-apology like an inexperienced adolescent.

"Let's go to the lab. But I warn you, you may not be able to logon right away. As I explained last night, your chemistry read-outs were so unusual, I don't know how long it will take the main computer to recalculate your blood values so that you may logon as YOU. If the Network doesn't recognize you, it will take me hours to find out what went wrong. Please, Nicolus, have patience."

Aura slipped by Nicolus in the doorway, leading him to the lab area in the dome, still coddling the exalted Macedonia. Macedonia obligingly vacated her arms as Aura began the reconnection procedure. She released the vein-plug from the soft under-belly of Nicolus' left wrist. The wrist unit offered resistance as Aura probed his vein for the metal contacts.

"Aura, are you getting even? Not now...not here," Nicolus playfully pleaded, exhibiting a twisted expression of obvious pain. The wrist unit finally surrendered to Aura's skilled manipulations, and snapped cleanly into the contacts. Finally, she attached the ribbon interface to the wrist unit, which ran from the main computer. The data transfer began.

"Darling, I never knew it could be so delicious," Nicolus said in a faked Greek accent as he caressed Aura's chin with his left hand, smiling a sensual, mischievous smile Aura had never witnessed in him before. His intentionally silky voice resonated throughout Aura's body. Nicolus held her with his dark eyes, momentarily distracting her. He knew of her long-suffering desire for him. He understood now, how she had been feeling.

Quickly averting her eyes, Aura continued to prime the wrist unit. Nicolus watched her every move with new, intense interest.

Motioning Nicolus to an examining platform, Aura said, "You have to wear this awhile. I'll come back in about an hour, meanwhile you relax and let nature take its course. You know."

Nicolus delighted in Aura's verbal mistake. Something very inviting was happening to him, something that he knew Aura was responding to with every cell in her body.

Determined not to allow Nicolus' unanticipated attraction to her interfere with the task at hand, Aura strode off into the main living quarters to find comfort in Macedonia's undemanding feline company.

\* \* \* \* \*

Aura lay limp on the cushdeck, her graying brown hair gracefully cascading down the dusty-rose velvet surface of the soft cushions, her pretty face conveying an almost hedonistic expression as pulses of electricity danced through her tired muscles. Macedonia purred shamelessly as he received second-hand current while resting on Aura's belly. The electrical stimulation treatments were becoming more frequent and necessary as Aura's one-hundred twenty-seven-year-old body responded less and less to them. Though she appeared a young forty-two, she was one of the few experimental subjects who had difficulty assimilating the RNA injections. Her own living cells, which she herself cultured some one-hundred two years ago, seemed to pervert during the long culturing process, and occasionally rejected reintroduction into her system. The soft electrical pulses from the cushdeck could gently encourage these cultured cells to release their RNA and renew Aura's vitality for a little longer—at least until the next treatment.

\* \* \* \* \* \*

In an hour, a refreshed Aura returned to the lab, focusing her gaze on the flurry of serum values madly scrolling up the screen. The transfer was nearly completed. She settled herself down at the keyboard and waited in silence, deliberately ignoring Nicolus as he lay there on the table, conspicuously studying her form.

He had never been this interested in Aura before. His personal aversion to (as well as the Foundation's unwritten rule against) intimacy with colleagues was disintegrating at an alarming rate. For the first time in over four years, working and living with Aura day to day, sharing professional challenges and the cargo of emotions inherent in scientific breakthroughs and abysmal failures...he wanted her.

"O.K., Nicolus, time to assess the damages," Aura said as she removed the cable from his wrist unit. From this point on, Aura was on her own, as Nicolus knew very little of hematology or interpreting serum values. He watched as she carefully scrutinized each screen of data, taking notice of any unusual changes.

"To be honest, this doesn't look good," Aura said. "Unless I can stabilize some of your hormones and neurotransmitters, and get them to come close to your previous levels, you won't be able to logon. The computer is just too sensitive to accept anything so radically different from your usual values. Some of this chemistry is really off....

"Uh...Nicolus, have you been feeling anything like you used to—like you used to feel before you started using the wrist unit? You may be at risk for one of those manic-depressive episodes you used to have." Aura shifted nervously in her chair as she went over the data. "According to your antibody screen, your immune system has also been weakened...and your...those can't be right," Aura said, as if she were the only one meant to hear it.

"We should run this again. Would you mind? It's only 6:20. We can get you straightened out by 8:00, the Foundation must be anxious."

"So am I," said Nicolus in a deliberately velvet voice as he slid himself off the examination table, reaching for Aura in an uncharacteristic spasm of sensual affection. Loyalty to the Foundation's rule—to himself—suddenly seemed unimportant virtues. His reluctance to have a sexual relationship with Aura simply evaporated as he held Aura's firm quaking body against his in a desperate, hungry embrace. He kissed her passionately, thoroughly immersed in the growing tension of pleasurable sensations long dormant in his years of self-denial. There was nothing he wanted more at this very moment than to share himself with Aura.

"Do you still want this, Aura? Do you still want me?" Nicolus asked her, continuing to caress her with his mouth.

Aura stared at him; he sensed her effort to deny her lust for him. He knew Aura; her love for him would never allow her to insist that he return it. Now he was offering himself to her, expecting a response. Not answering, she took his right hand and led him into her quarters.

As Nicolus closed the door behind them, Macedonia scrambled towards Aura's room, aiming for the last visible crack in the doorway. He collided clumsily with the door as it clicked shut. Insulted, he resignedly flopped outside the door and patiently awaited Aura's exit. Minutes, then hours passed as he absorbed Aura's complex array of emotional rapture. Macedonia had never experienced such rare pleasure. He stretched out, and purred, passively assimilating every tender feeling, every fervent arousal, every wave of gratification. The alien sensations frolicked in his feline mind. He was indescribably happy.

The door to Aura's room creaked open, and Nicolus' naked body stepped out first, his foot just grazing Macedonia's exposed, supine belly. "Jesus, I almost squashed your cat. What's he doing, anyway?

Aura, is he sick or something?" Nicolus asked, genuinely concerned.

Aura stared down at the ridiculously prostrated feline. "Oh God, that must have been one hell of a confusing experience." Aura stated flatly. "Are you alright boy? I didn't even stop to think what this could do to you." Aura knelt down to pet Macedonia.

"What? You mean...." Nicolus stammered in a half whisper as he considered what Aura just said. "Did he...did he pick up on all that... did he actually feel what you felt when—when we...?" Nicolus' mouth hung partially open as his thoughts raced.

"I guess so, Nicolus. You just made love with me—and Macedonia. What talent you possess, lover."

"Jesus, four years of celibacy, and I turn into a pervert! Isn't there any way to turn him off?" Nicolus asked anxiously.

"No, it's permanent. The Cognitive Binary Translator implant is now an integral part of his brain, that's how he knows what I'm thinking and feeling. Sometimes I wish I could turn him off. The Foundation briefed me about death—how he would be capable of experiencing my last thoughts up until the end. But sex. No one told me about sex. I guess they didn't feel they had to. I am expected to honor the non-intimacy code just as you are. This is history-making as far as Macedonia is concerned. How we could document it without incurring the wrath of the Foundation, I don't know. Someday, someone will, and it should be us—if we want to stay in the limelight." Nicolus listened in amazement as Aura droned on about how fantastic it was that her companion had experienced something supposedly no other cat had ever experienced: human sexuality—a mind fuck.

\* \* \* \* \* \*

Feeling disturbed and somehow betrayed, or worse—violated, Nicolus made his way to the kitchen. His stride was abruptly stopped by the irritating whine of the dome page. Someone was requesting admittance.

In a blur of bare skin, Nicolus and Aura dashed into Aura's quarters, just remembering to leap over the still upside down and writhing Macedonia. Nicolus dressed with uncommon speed, and hastily made his way to the front entrance. The shriek of the dome page continued to rip into his whirling mind. He stood there, catching his breath, calming himself, reassuring himself that no one could possibly be able to tell what had transpired between Aura and him over the last six hours.

"Yes, may we know your name and purpose of this visit?" Nicolus asked officially as he spoke into the intercom near the entrance.

"This is Lieutenant General Bailey from the Foundation. I'm here to see Nicolus Teal. He hasn't reported in two days," growled the authoritative voice from outside.

Nicolus' repressed fears of the previous night surfaced with a vengeance. Nicolus whipped around to lock gazes with a frozen, bug-eyed Aura. He opened the door, and offered his right hand to the Lt. General in greeting. Nicolus forced an insincere smile as he gestured the uniformed and adorned dignitary to the cushdeck to be seated.

As the huge man loomed near, Macedonia slipped under the cushdeck to hide. Not acknowledging the cat's indiscretion, Nicolus spoke confidently. "Sir, I am Nicolus Teal. What brings a busy and important person such as yourself to our dome?"

Removing his black-lensed sun shields, The Lt. General spoke. "Dr. Teal, the Foundation has informed me that you have not logged-on in two days. Is there a problem? Perhaps we may be of assist...."

"No—there's no problem, at least nothing we can't handle," Nicolus lied in his cool, detached manner. Inside, his adrenaline saturated body conspired to expose his deception. How he wished the wrist unit would kick in and quell his nearly intolerable agitation.

"The wrist unit has recently demonstrated some peculiar changes," Nicolus continued. "Dr. Maitland and I are currently analyzing these changes and should be reporting our observations soon. It's nothing serious."

"Changes? What do you mean by 'changes'?" The Lt. General seemed to show special interest in Nicolus' non-committal description of the problem.

"Well, sir," Nicolus said, clearing his throat, "some of my lab values have become slightly distorted and, knowing how sensitive the Network biological passcodes are, I didn't feel I would be able to logon until Aura—Dr. Maitland, and I had remedied the problem."

"You didn't even try? How do you know you can't logon if you never tried?" bellowed Lt. General Bailey. "Logon, Dr. Teal!" The Lt. General's squinty blue eyes narrowed as his bushy gray eyebrows folded into them, half burying the pupils in a landscape of senile foliage.

Truly rattled now, Nicolus fought to maintain his facade of composure. He glanced over to Aura, who sat stiff and silent, propped on the edge of the cushdeck.

Suddenly, a strange smacking noise pierced the momentary silence. Visibly distracted, the Lt. General demanded, "What in the world is that noise?"

Embarrassed, Aura dropped her gaze and softly answered, "It's Macedonia. Whenever he gets nervous, he hides under the cushdeck and sucks his tail." Aura forced a phony snicker.

"Isn't that the cat that has the CBT implant?" asked the Lt. General.

"Yes, that's him. He was the finest of his group—save for a few annoying habits," Aura apologized.

"And just who is he calibrated to- you, or Dr. Teal?" the Lt. General interrogated.

"Me, sir," Aura quickly answered. It would be far more acceptable to the Lt. General that Macedonia continued to slurp and suck under the cushdeck as a result of her nervousness. Any obvious nervousness in Nicolus could have revealed that he was in fact lying and covering up.

Several minutes dragged on. Lt. General Bailey seemed satisfied with the lengthy explanations of their "minor problems" with the wrist unit, and got up to leave. "Don't you worry about those distorted values. Logon. I'll tell the Board you'll be filing a complete report soon. They'll be expecting your comments." Lt. General Bailey let himself out.

\* \* \* \* \* \*

"What a friggin' son-of-a-bitch asshole. . . !" Nicolus spewed, clutching his head and pulling his hair through his fingers. "I can't believe how stupid these higher-ups are. All they do is sit at their friggin' desk, filling out their friggin' forms. They have no understanding of how the machines that they lord over, make laws about, and have us create impossible passcodes for...even work!" Nicolus angrily paced through the main quarters of the dome, trying to expend the wash of adrenaline scouring his veins.

"Hey, Nicolus. Think about it. You didn't tell him how serious the problem was. How else could he react? He doesn't know what you know, you made sure of that. Calm down. Want a drink, or would you rather have an injection? This doctor is insisting you do one or the other. Your wrist unit must still be malfunctioning. You may have looked calm on the outside when that pompous ass was here, but I know better." Aura folded her arms around his sweat-soaked shoulders and kissed him delicately.

Nicolus returned her affection in a forceful, insistent way, his anger evolving into urgent sexual desire.

"Nicolus...take it easy," Aura complained.

Relaxing his hug, Nicolus smiled seductively as he impatiently unzipped the front of Aura's gown, exposing her naked femaleness from her full breasts to the middle of her thighs. Her knees weakened as Nicolus tongued every inch of her. In unison, they sank to the floor, forgetting where they were and the recent visit of the Foundation emissary. In a fit of passion, Nicolus frantically ripped his gown over his head, forgetting it too had a front zipper, and finished Aura—spending himself—there on the floor of the main quarters of the dome. Macedonia yowled a throaty Siamese caterwaul.

"Well said," puffed Nicolus as he lay naked and enervated beside Aura. Macedonia's involuntary voyeurism no longer disturbed him.

"I don't know what's gotten into you, Nicolus. But whatever it is, I like what's gotten into me," Aura joked as she gazed at Nicolus. "You know, we have a hell of a lot of work to do. What are we doing laying on the floor, screwing our brains out, when you're about to have a chunk of your ass removed by those jerks at the Foundation?"

With that reminder, Nicolus pushed to his feet and, grabbing his gown, made his way to the wall unit.

\* \* \* \* \* \*

Nicolus designed the wall unit over eight years ago when he was still attending The University. A roomful of various electronics was neatly installed in a four-foot wide, three-foot tall unit, counter-sunk into the wall. On the small desk beneath the wall unit sat a keyboard for typed commands to the computer (if voice activation wasn't appropriate or desirable) and a stack of notebooks and logs Nicolus had spent years filling in during his affiliation with the Foundation.

With the exception of the Foundation supported labor class who built and maintained everything, most people worked at home, in research (biological and technological), in art and design, and in journalism. No one owned software as in years before, but shared the use of the Network's vast library of applications, storing their own data on the Foundation's huge Crystal RAM unit. There could be no theft of data, no plagiarism, no pirating of applications software.

It was the wrist unit which Nicolus and Aura had developed, that made all of this possible. It was a marvel of micro-engineering, no more than an inch in diameter and less than an eighth of an inch thick. With the exception of very few, everyone in the colony, droid worker and Network user alike, was required to wear one.

The earlier prototypes were designed to administer medication at regular intervals. In the years that followed the device gained sophistication in monitoring vital signs, blood chemistry and neural activity. It could be programmed to automatically adjust medication dosage (and even administer drugs which could never before breach the blood-brain barrier.), alter neurotransmitter imbalances (as Nicolus' own wrist unit once did in stabilizing his manic-depression episodes), and wake a sleeper at the time appropriate to his chemistry: when his blood values showed the optimal time to be awake. Because Circadian rhythms necessarily would change the time of the wake up stimulant infusion day to day, the work-force was active at all hours. This staggering of the work-force increased efficiency and productivity by seven hundred percent.

The advanced wrist unit module worn by those using the Network was an integral part of logon procedure, matching antibody panels, blood type and neurotransmitter activity to Foundation archive samples. Security was of utmost importance. No unauthorized person could access the Network; within a narrow range, any deviance would result in denial of access. Anyone having a cold could expect to be denied. Anyone under extreme stress could expect to be denied. Anyone...like Nicolus, could expect to be denied.

\* \* \* \* \*

Nicolus sat at the keyboard, growing increasingly negative as he pondered how he would fool the Network into accepting his logon. "You know, I have nothing to say to those bastards...Nothing. I'm not ready to tell them all that has been happening the last two days—that the wrist unit is not functioning, that I was in a coma, that I am about to have a nervous breakdown, that I've been balling my colleague like I was some kind of sex maniac. Why am I sitting here torturing myself?" Nicolus thought out loud.

Resigning himself to the inevitable, Nicolus removed the wrist unit and plugged it into the wall unit. He keyed in his passcode and pressed the 'enter' key. A few seconds passed, and the words, PLEASE WAIT. . . appeared on the screen. The instructions, PLEASE VOICE ID, prompted Nicolus to speak his name and title into the microphone, then press 'enter'. PLEASE WAIT. . . .

PLEASE STAND. . . . A small lens above the screen opened to snap a shot of his irritated, worried face. PLEASE FINGERPRINT ID. . . . Nicolus placed his hand on the monitor and with the other, pressed the 'enter' key.

A full three minutes passed as Nicolus cursed beneath his breath.

The damned system is frozen up, he thought. He knew it was pointless to go on. The computer was probably trying to match the blood values from the wrist unit, found that they didn't even remotely correspond to his archive readings, and was preparing to close down on him. Jumping up from his seat, he was startled by Aura's high-pitched voice.

"Look, Nicolus, you're in!"

"What the hell? How can that be?" Nicolus' face was slack and blank. Baffled, he reseated himself. He slowly leaned toward the goosenecked microphone, and tried to speak, staring at the waiting screen, completely astonished that he had got that far.

"Nicolus Teal, AI bio-unit one four six," he carefully articulated. "Report-update, by order of Lieutenant General Bailey, Wednesday, Spring fifty-sixth, Three-Hundred Ninety-Nine, Antares Five star-time."

Nicolus drew a deep, cleansing breath, wondering what he would say next, groping for the right words: words that would say as little as possible but sound impressive to the Board.

"My wrist unit has apparently malfunctioned, somewhat affecting my sleep-wake cycle," Nicolus lied. "Due to the consequent disturbances in my circadian rhythm, my serum values became—understandably—distorted. I did not expect to be able to logon until Dr. Maitland and I had corrected the problem. The fact that I have in fact logged on, attests to the triviality of the problem. When we have finished our analysis of the wrist unit we will report our findings to the Board. Until that time, we do not find it necessary or advisable to issue any recall of the unit, or news of this incident. Our current research project will be suspended until further notice." What a bucket of bilge, Nicolus thought, logging-off.

Nicolus smiled slyly as he sauntered over to the cushdeck where Aura sat witnessing his verbal deceptions. His apparent conquest of an insurmountable problem was a soothing salve for his tired mind. Aura took his hand, then kissed him lightly on the cheek.

"Congratulations. You're more full of shit than a chem-waste dump."

"Well, what happens next? We really do have to find out what's wrong with the wrist unit—and fast. We can't keep avoiding the Foundation's drilling investigations. Sending someone out here—a General of all people—to check up on me was so unlike their standard procedure that I wonder just what really is going on. They could have called. Why didn't they? Doesn't that bother you, Aura?" Nicolus bounced his questions off her. "And how in the world could I logon with NO difficulty at all? Last year, when I had that virus, I was forbidden access for almost three weeks. If it hadn't been for you and your biochemical magic, I wouldn't have been able to use the system for months. And now...now. It doesn't make sense."

"Let's get to work then. Get your wrist unit and bring it to the lab. We'll tear it down to the last neural connection if we have to," Aura reassured him.

They worked until midnight, assisted by intelligent programmable microscopes and probes Nicolus had designed years ago, picking at every last chip and neural connection. "I can't find anything wrong enough to account for your coma and your ongoing problems with physiological regulation, Nicolus," stated Aura. "The drug delivery system seems to be operating fine, the neural and blood sensors are functioning...we've tested everything except the programming unit. That, Dear Nicolus, is your domain. You're on your own."

"Tomorrow. My neck is killing me." Nicolus stiffly started back to his quarters, when he stopped and wheeled around. "I never thought I'd ever be asking you this, but would you like to sleep with me ?"

Smiling warmly, Aura went to him and hugged him, accepting his offer. Nicolus rested in Aura's arms, reveling in the almost forgotten splendor of being held by a woman while he slept.

Aura awoke just after dawn, and peering down at Nicolus peaceful sleeping face, began to frantically shake him, calling out his name.

"Huh...what's you're problem?" Nicolus asked groggily as he rolled over on his side to face Aura. "What time is it?"

"Jesus, I had this hideous flashback of when...I'm sorry. Go back to sleep if you like." Tears squeezed into her eyes as she looked at Nicolus. "It's 5:45," Aura remembered to say, leaving his quarters.

\* \* \* \* \* \*

Nicolus whisked past Aura at her work bench in the lab. "How long will it take you to reassemble the wrist unit?"

"About an hour, I guess. Why?" Aura's quizzical face glowed in the green wash of the work bench lighting.

"I'm going to logon again. I'm going to tell those assholes what we've found up till now. That'll keep them away from the dome—I hope. The more I think about yesterday's intrusion, the madder I get. They're never supposed to go to the researchers' domes without announcing it. Did you hear the phone page, Aura?"

Shaking her head no, Aura slumped in her chair.

Nicolus boomed, "Neither did I!" He hesitated for a moment, then added, "I think I may even ask for a raise. No—I'll demand one!" Reluctantly, Aura began putting the wrist unit back together. "What a relief it'll be to have the sure, confident, controlled and cooperative Nicolus back," she muttered under her breath. Nicolus was approaching the manic phase of his medical condition. As much as Aura enjoyed making love with the impulsive, reckless side of him, his concentration was suffering. And so was his judgement.

"Oh, Nicolus—remember we have to prime the unit when you put it back on. That'll take another hour, like before," Aura reminded him.

Nicolus rushed out of the lab, seemingly charged with energy he couldn't expend. His mind churned with ideas, possibilities, suspicions, accusations. Feelings of distrust and persecution whittled away at his reason. He hated the Foundation for their audacious interference in his important work—in his very life. How dare they send a General to the dome unannounced! They had no right to scare me like that! It was none of their business if I had sex with my colleague—who was responsible for this rule, anyway?

Slamming his fist onto the kitchen counter, he spotted Macedonia scurrying from under the cushdeck. Regaining a semblance of calm, he said, "Have you been under there all night? Huh, Macedonia? Why can't you understand me?"

Nicolus shuffled through the tins of cat food stored in the overhead cabinet, looking for something a cat might want for breakfast. "Braised Beef, Roast Horse-Meat...Veal Parmigiana? Don't they ever can anything that cats like...like shrew, cricket, or day-old road-coat? Jesus, this stuff was canned for people, not cats. Ever seen Kitty dragging home a steer carcass?" Nicolus mused to himself to pass the time.

Macedonia listened to him, watched him intently, cocking his head occasionally as if accenting each of Nicolus' silly ramblings.

Nicolus generously heaped a tin of Braised Beef on Macedonia's plate, then went back to the lab.

\* \* \* \* \* \*

Nicolus impatiently fidgeted while Aura disconnected the interface ribbon. His wrist unit recalculated, he quickly made his way to the main quarters. Following standard logon procedures, he waited patiently to gain access to the Foundation Network. A blue flash shocked Nicolus' eyes as a familiar but unexpected Foundation logo splashed onto the monitor. Another screen blinked on:

MANDATORY PERIODIC RANDOM TESTING

Nicolus felt a wave of nausea spill from his guts into every throbbing tissue of his body. "Aura—get out here!" he yelled, unable to unlock his gaze from the monitor screen.

Aura rushed to his side. Her eyes darted from Nicolus' distressed face to the blue screen. "My God! Not now!" she gasped.

"What am I going to do? I can't take their damned competency tests in my condition! I need something. Please, Aura can you give me something?" Nicolus nervously fiddled with his gown zipper as beads of sweat glistened on his upper lip and forehead.

"No—the drug hits too hard. It takes about thirty minutes to level off. You'll either have to take the test now, or risk some real shit if you log-off," Aura said.

Nicolus sucked in deep lungfuls of air as Aura rubbed his tense neck and back muscles.

The test was miserable and tedious, as it had been on other occasions, but now infiltrated with doses of fear and trepidation. Nicolus fought to maintain his poise as he was sequentially tested in concentration, recall, speed and reasoning. His mind was confused, sluggish and sometimes irrational; he sensed this with each error. A tremor developed in his hands as he drove himself to answer the questions scrolling on the screen. Number four...true...false...yes...no. Nicolus typed in answers to endless questions, becoming more unsure of their accuracy. It shouldn't be this hard, Nicolus worried. I've passed these tests twice yearly for almost four years. I have never failed; I am not going to fail now.

His mind involuntarily interrupted his focus with images of Aura's curvy, naked body, her face when she...Then—Macedonia. The General. Macedonia devouring the General. He battled with his own mind to concentrate. Then, at last, it was over.

Nicolus sat silently; the blank screen seemed to ridicule him. In a blink, a new screen appeared, assessing Nicolus' scores:

```
MPRT SCORE: > NICOLUS TEAL, AI BIO-UNIT 146/
ANTARES FIVE STAR-TIME 399/S57

> CONCENTRATION:   32
 > RECALL:   98
> SPEED:   102
> REASONING:   66
```

VALUES BELOW 85% OF LAST SCORE ARE UNACCEPTABLE>
THE FOUNDATION RESERVES THE RIGHT TO TERMINATE
ALL PERSONNEL NOT COMPLYING WITH REGULATION
55.62A/303—EFFICIENCY STANDARDS

Thoroughly demoralized, Nicolus left the wall unit and quietly retired to his quarters. Aura retrieved the wrist unit and, following him, secured it to Nicolus' wrist. His energy of the early morning was drained from him. He stared, without emotion, into Aura's brown eyes, not wanting to say or do anything.

"We'll find it, Nicolus," Aura reassured him, fondling his hair. "We'll find out what's wrong with the wrist unit and get you back on track. Unfortunately, what's left to do involves your expertise, and right now I don't think you're in any shape to proceed just yet. You should rest a bit." Aura left him with his thoughts.

Staring at the right-hand wall for some time, Nicolus caught a glimpse of Aura returning to his quarters. He turned his head and quietly spoke. "Did you see what happened? That wasn't me out there—I never fail these tests—never. I just couldn't concentrate, couldn't focus on a damned thing. Weird images kept creeping into my mind—sex, death, gore—bizarre crap I shouldn't have been thinking. I'm finished. I'll bet the Board found the results and is already stacking up shipping crates for me. I can't believe how lucky I could be to logon this day, under these circumstances and get my ass quizzed. I already passed twice this...." Nicolus gulped as his eyes widened in realization. "I've already been tested twice this year! Those bastards! They can't test me again—not until next year. Those test results are invalid. Aura, they can't use them!" Nicolus sprung from his bed and charged to the lab.

Nicolus ripped the wrist unit from his arm, dripping blood on the work bench as he jammed the unit into the main computer. He typed in commands to retrieve the wrist unit's medical programming section. He scrutinized each line with uncommon patience.

Two hours passed before Nicolus emerged from the lab, his face drained of expression as well as color. He walked to the kitchen area and poured a cup of sweet ethanol. Aura watched him as he downed almost ten ounces of eighty proof liquor.

"Hey, easy with that stuff, it can impair your vision. Who's going to analyze the wrist unit programs if you're wearing flannel glasses?"

"No one. It's done," Nicolus said in an uninspired monotone.

"Done? Well, what did you find out?" Aura asked anxiously.

Nicolus stalled, searching for the words, trying to avoid alarming

Aura. "Aura, I think I love you," he said evasively.

"How's the fucking program?" Aura's voice deepened in anger. She had barely noticed what he said.

"The program's been changed. It's not mine. Someone changed it—radically. Aura, I've been sabotaged," Nicolus said dryly.

"What? Changed—how? How bad is it?" Aura asked in disbelief. She placed her hands on her mouth as she tried to understand the hidden, unstated meaning lurking in Nicolus' blatantly unemotional answer. The next questions would be unaskable.

Calmly, Aura began gushing an endless string of ideas, hoping Nicolus would grab onto one and do something with it. He rejected everything she said.

"I don't want to talk right now. I'm going to logon."

"Bombed? You know damn well you can't logon pickled. Besides, the wrist unit has been disconnected from you for over two and a half hours—a half hour over the limit. It'll have to be recalculated. Nicolus, are you crazy?" Aura reprimanded him.

"No—I'm dangerous."

Nicolus took Aura's arm and towed her into the lab. "Recalc, please," he ordered her.

\* \* \* \* \* \*

Nicolus was at the wall unit, grinning foolishly, obviously quite drunk as the face ID camera took his picture. He finished his logon and sat, waiting, strangely confident, very sure of his hunch. The introduction screen popped up:

```
NICOLUS TEAL AI BIO-UNIT 146 ANTARES
          STAR TIME 399/S57.
          ACCESS GRANTED
```

Standing behind Nicolus, Aura suddenly blurted, "Log-off! Log-off!"

"Yeah, why the hell not? I can get in anytime. Under any conditions—sick, asleep, ripped, drugged. Dead. I think next time I'll get creative...stand on my head, maybe wear rubber gloves. Maybe I'll let you get me all hot, then rush in here and logon while I come. That should change something," Nicolus said.

"Yeah, like your residence," Aura quipped. Aura suggested that she logon, since she hadn't for at least a month. She waited as the computer compared her logon data with the Foundation's archive values. The computer beeped, the monitor flipped screens and the words `ACCESS DENIED` appeared in the center of the screen. Aura sat motionless, not especially surprised.

"I'll bet the changes in my hormones since we've been...." Aura's voice trailed off.

"But what about my hormones? Mine have to be changed too. Why can I get in, but you can't? I'm no more important to the Foundation than you are."

"I don't know Nicolus. This is how the program is supposed to work. That's the way you wrote it. It's supposed to deny access to everyone who may be operating at substandard efficiency due to illness, stress or overwork, as well as prevent unauthorized access. No offense, but there must be something wrong with the main access program. You'll have to rewrite it—make security even tighter than it is now." Aura explained her concerns with he program, trying not to offend Nicolus in his morally marooned state.

"There's nothing wrong with my program!" Nicolus roared. "The Foundation has been using it for years—those pukes at the Foundation bitch and whine, always wanting more from you than you can give, and half the time they don't even pay you for any revisions! It would take weeks to go through the program. I'm NOT going to do it! There's nothing wrong with my program! It's perfect—perfect!"

Nicolus knew she had heard it all before many times, but not quite so explosively. It is exactly the response that she must have expected from him, however loaded with irrational emotion it was. She had worked with him on the program; he could never have written it without her medical knowledge. In a fit of egotistical jealousy, he forgot that. For just an instant, it was his program. Nicolus felt remorse as Aura just sat there, expressionless, glaring at him knowingly.

\* \* \* \* \* \*

The next day, a sober and collected Nicolus logged-on several times without any difficulty. The ID camera zoomed in on his carefully positioned bare ass, once. Another time, the fingerprint ID accepted surgical-gloved fingers without question.

The ring of the phone page ended Nicolus' frivolous fun.

"Nicolus Teal, Dr. Nicolus Teal?" a feminine voice inquired. "Please activate your view screen."

There before him was the aged, box-like face of Lt. General Bailey. "Dr. Teal, why have you logged-on several times today, accessing none of the libraries, and leaving no reports? We need your report regarding the malfunctions of the wrist unit. When may we expect it?"

Bloated, dictatorial bastard, thought Nicolus. "Aura and I are currently disassembling the unit. We have not yet been able to discern the cause of the problems. Please bear with us. We are doing the best we can."

"Aura...you mean Dr. Maitland, don't you?" the Lt. General sneered.

"Yes, Dr. Maitland." Nicolus almost swallowed his tongue when he realized his slip-up. Colleagues are never referred to by their first names, otherwise the relationship could be considered something more than professional.

"By the way," Nicolus said, risking losing his temper. "Why was I tested yesterday? I have already been tested twice this year, and passed admirably, I might add."

The Lt. General removed his gaze, mumbled something, then said, "I have no knowledge of your being retested. I'll look into it. Meanwhile, get that report ready. Sign off." The view screen faded to gray.

He was lying his dentures out; Nicolus knew it. A liar can always spot another liar. Nicolus began to feel even more distrustful and suspicious. There was something going on in the Federation— something big, something he couldn't...wouldn't be told. He was determined to find out what it was; he had to. He felt any day he would lose his mind completely.

His original idea of feeding the Foundation daily tidbits of information on the wrist unit would have to be modified. He was now fighting for his own preservation. He didn't want them to know about the corrupted medprog in his own wrist unit; he couldn't explain how it had happened anyway. As far as Nicolus knew, he was the only neural-computer programmer living in the colony. Right now he needed Aura, her caresses, her warm body, her love. He wanted her to love him. It was a foreign want, but so necessary to his waning sanity. He replaced his wrist unit and left to find her.

Nicolus stood at the entrance to the lab, watching Aura flip through her manuals. She was lovely. She was absolutely the most beautiful woman he had ever known. He really did love her, he confessed to himself. He silently crept up behind her, reaching around to fill his hands with her breasts.

"God, Nicolus, aren't you supposed to be analyzing the medical program in the wrist unit?" Aura asked, irritated at his untimely, unsolicited overtures.

"Can't you get away for just a short while?" he begged, flirting with his eyes.

"Was that the Lt. General's voice I heard? You really should be getting your ass in gear," Aura said. "I think I should start you on hypodermic medication for awhile; it'll help your concentration. It's all I can do for you until you fix the wrist unit program."

Nicolus felt rejected for a second, then, sighing deeply, shrugged an answer. "That is my job, Dear Aura, to concentrate. Go ahead."

It took hours before Nicolus realized that his mind was beginning to clear. The tangle of confusion and several days of mental fog was lifting, exposing the orderly, logical Nicolus he thought he had lost for good. Everything began to make sense again. He knew what he had to do.

Confident and determined, he immediately logged-on to the Network, intending to reveal everything to the Foundation. He had no other logical choice; they had to know. He sat calmly at the microphone, methodically detailing the last few days' events. As he confided his concerns that others may also be affected, that the entire work-force and even official users could be "infected" by this unknown saboteur, his words re-entered his mind, amplifying and confirming the gravity of the situation. Had there been any complaints of drug overdose or shutdown of medication delivery? Had there been any reports of coma or temper flare-ups? Nicolus avoided discussing his unusually ravenous sexual appetite—he couldn't risk it. His loyalty to the Foundation returned to him, compelling him to admit that there may be a problem with the main logon program.

"And in conclusion, I wish to add that after I have repaired the medprog in my own wrist unit, I will be implementing a complete revision of the logon program. Our people must not suffer as I have suffered. I await your report as to the extent of the spread of wrist unit complications within the colony." Brilliant. The ball's back in their court, and I'm off the hook for awhile, Nicolus thought.

\* \* \* \* \* \*

The days passed quickly as Nicolus spent hour after hour absorbed in scanning and re-writing the lines in his medical program. Whoever did this, he thought, was an amateur. It was a sloppy entanglement of spaghetti code at best; at worst a deliberate bungle meant to kill the user. A wave of nauseated relief passed over him as he appreciated just how close he had come to death. He wondered if any of the other colonists had been affected; the Foundation had not reported any cases as yet.

Reasoning he needed Aura to complete the medical adjustments, he headed for her quarters. Waking her would be difficult.

She slept curled up with Macedonia under her chin. "Aura," he said as he gently rocked her shoulders.

Macedonia woke and stretched, rubbing his body against Nicolus' arm in a semi-conscious haze.

"Not now, Nicolus, I'm tired," Aura moaned.

"I need your help in the lab. The program's ready to be impregnated with the medical data. I don't know what I'm doing," Nicolus explained.

"No—you can do it. Just use the manuals. Those figures are close enough. I'll fine tune them for you later."

Nicolus was surprised at her lack of concern, even reluctance to help. He went back to the lab, not particularly upset at her, but not especially looking forward to typing in all the numbers. He wasn't really familiar enough with them to be able to catch errors. How strange that Aura would dump it on me like that, he thought.

\* \* \* \* \* \*

Aura woke late in the evening, and vaguely remembering that Nicolus had rousted her earlier, went to the lab to see how he was doing. He wasn't there.

Nicolus looked up from his questionable culinary concoction, chewing thoughtfully, as Aura staggered into the kitchen.

"How's the program coming?" she asked.

"Terrific. I'm done. I need a recalc now. Gotta logon and tell the Board that Phase One is completed."

"Phase One?" Aura asked.

"Yeah. Phase Two is rewriting the logon program," Nicolus stated succinctly.

Aura sat down at the table across from him. "So you're going to do it...you're really going to do it?"

"Better safe than...anyway it would be immoral to let this thing get out of hand. The whole colony could be affected. Maybe it has already, and the Foundation is up to it's armpits in...."

"Since when have you had morals?" Aura teased, referring to his active libido.

"Since when have you lost yours?" Nicolus snapped back. "Why did you leave me holding the bag in the lab? I could have really goofed."

"Did you? I believed you would be fine. I had faith in your ability and precision. If you can write a program, you can type in numbers from a medical manual. I'll tailor the figures to your individual needs when you get the logon program fixed," Aura said.

Still troubled at her lack of concern, Nicolus finished his meal. He walked over to Aura and, using her shoulder as a pivot point, motioned towards the lab with his head.

After the recalculating process, Aura asked, "And just how do you plan to keep the integrity of the medical program when you logon? Won't it get screwed up again like before?"

"Not a chance. I've added a subroutine to prevent tampering. It's tighter than a virgin sitting in a puddle of alum." Nicolus went on to explain, as best as he could to a non-programmer, how he had rigged the program with hidden instructions to prevent over-writing or revision. Aura listened, eyes glazed over, appearing lost in the technical details.

"But how will I be able to fine tune it, if it's locked up?" Aura asked.

"It'll be a bitch, but I can unlock it—when the time comes."

\* \* \* \* \* \*

Nicolus closed his report to the Foundation: "I have succeeded in repairing my wrist unit's medprog to full function. I should be feeling the effects in a few hours. I will begin rewriting the logon program tomorrow. Please arrange for Special Security Access Download. I estimate the time required to complete this project to be three weeks maximum." Nicolus thought for a few moments, then added, "Also, please submit to me any reports regarding malfunctions in other wrist units. I will re-program them as needed."

\* \* \* \* \* \*

Nicolus was awakened by the tingle of mild stimulant infusion from the wrist unit. It was working perfectly. He lingered in his bed, smiling to himself as he looked around at his collections of photographs hanging on every wall, not really seeing them in the dim light, but recalling the memories of them. He did not have difficulty in adjusting to the medications from the wrist unit, as he feared he might. Things are going to be O.K.—I'm going to make it, he decided. I'll have to tell Aura, she'll be glad. He felt like going into her room and...no, he didn't, really. It was a nice idea, but he had important work to do.

\* \* \* \* \* \*

Two weeks advanced as Nicolus examined every line of the Foundation's main logon program, searching for flaws, inversions, transpositions, additions—anything that could give him a clue as to how a saboteur could access the Network, jumbling Nicolus' and perhaps others' medical programs by feeding back an altered medprog into the wrist unit.

He forgot to eat; sometimes he forgot to feed Macedonia (but not for long). Even though the three week deadline was near, he enjoyed being immersed in his work, revising, refining and testing every line. His anger with the Foundation was behind him, buried in the distant fog of those few insane days. Everything was in balance.

Aura, however, was another matter. She was becoming more irritable as Nicolus thwarted her sexual come-ons day after day. She became accusatory, demanding and irrational at times. Nicolus regarded her behavior with nothing more than curiosity. On the rare occasions that he did succumb to her sexual coaxing, his passion was gentle, subdued, even disinterested. Nicolus still craved Aura's loving hugs and kisses, but felt no compulsion to consummate the affection between them.

His cycle now approaching Aura's—but still off by two hours, Nicolus dragged his tired body to his bed and flopped face down on the fluffy blue blanket. He had been arguing—if you can call it that—with Aura about sex again. (She somehow had a talent for arguing with herself.) Nicolus had just nodded his head and smiled, saying, "I understand. Please calm down, Darling."

Her words ricocheted inside his brain. "And another thing—your work has lost its pizzazz too. Why did you lose interest—what's the Foundation Board going to say? You went into it with all you had, and now...all you do is eat and stare out the shutters at that hideous red sun." He had suggested maybe he was coming down with a "stop-and smell-the-roses" virus, but that went over like a turd in a punch bowl.

Her ranting continued to bounce off the inside of his cranium. "There's nothing wrong with you, your lab values are fine! You shouldn't be having these problems!"

Why did she feel so bad about how good he felt? The Foundation hadn't reported any wrist unit malfunctions, any uncontrolled tempers, or any comas. So what if he took his sweet time revising the logon program? Nicolus laughed, muffling his mirth in the blanket.

Lying there, he suddenly realized that he hadn't eaten in several hours. He wandered to the kitchen, thinking of what he might eat that didn't require preparation. Out of the corner of his right eye, as he passed the lab, he caught a glimpse of Aura sitting in the green light of the work bench, Macedonia in her lap.

Nicolus reversed, and stood to the side of the partially closed lab door; he watched unnoticed. A long ribbon interface cable ran from the computer to the back of Macedonia's skull. Nicolus squinted his eyes, trying to discern the words scrolling up the screen. They were lines to a program...a program? It was a strangely familiar program. Intrigued, Nicolus furtively stepped inside the lab—straining to see the screen without alerting Aura. Macedonia sat obediently, attentively on Aura's lap, the interface dangling from his head. Aura typed in new program lines—over-writing and replacing existing ones.

Jolted by revelation, Nicolus dared not breathe. He retreated in horror to the outside of the lab door. His heart raced, he tried to pant inaudibly as his lungs cried for more air. Nicolus felt sick and weak as the images bludgeoned his mind. Aura was changing a medical program—his medical program, and she was using the cat to do it!

My God, I've been fucking the saboteur! Nicolus' mind was a snarl of thoughts coming in at lightening speed. My head wasn't up my ass, it was between her legs. What could she be doing...and why?

The wrist unit kicked into high gear, injecting small spurts of Nicolus' medication into his surging bloodstream. A welcome calm washed through his veins, soaked into his reeling brain. Gradually, rational thought prevailed as he planned his approach to Aura's treachery.

\* \* \* \* \* \*

Nicolus lay in his bed in the dark, thinking everything through. Aura's lack of concern, the Lt. General's visit,—and Macedonia. It wasn't his imagination the cat was acting strange—staring at Nicolus as he often did. What could it all mean? Nicolus knew now that he had to finish the logon program—to stop Aura from messing with his medical program.

Funny, Nicolus thought, I almost admire her for her cleverness. I never had a clue—I never in my wildest imagination would have guessed it was her fooling with the wrist unit programs. She was so warm and supportive, so cool and seductive. Was it some sort of secret project or a desperate long-shot? His mind exhausted from unanswerable questions, he closed his eyes and willed himself to sleep, putting aside Aura's treason until the morning. Yes, morning will come soon enough, Aura.

\* \* \* \* \* \*

Confident and secure in his plan to trap Aura, Nicolus went to the kitchen for breakfast. Aura was already sitting at the table, eating and reading print-outs.

"Good morning," Nicolus said pleasantly. "Sleep well?"

"Yeah, I usually do," Aura said as she folded the sheets of data and placed them on her lap.

"Where's Macedonia? He's usually sitting here glaring at me."

"He's around here somewhere, you know how he is, " Aura answered, not looking up from her plate.

"Why does the Foundation use cats for telepathy studies, anyway? Why not dogs, or cockatoos, or something more cooperative?" Nicolus was getting excited as he began his slow mental torture of Aura.

"For one thing, cats' brains are a uniform size and weight from about six months of age on. Kittens respond favorably because they look upon their human companions as parents. True, some cats outgrow that attachment, but most never do. When we get them translating as kittens, they're usually locked in for life. Siamese cats in particular are known for their need for human interaction. Cats are discriminating; they rarely form casual alliances.

"Dogs, on the other hand, don't do well as CBT subjects, not only because of differing brain sizes, but also because they often look upon humans as playmates, pack members, or even possessions to be guarded. Dogs are not as clean as cats, and require more care than cats. Cats are the logical choice."

"That's interesting, I never knew that before. Has a CBT cat ever been calibrated to more than one human at a time?" He watched Aura carefully as he skillfully challenged her calmness.

Aura looked up suddenly. "Why would you ask that?"

"Macedonia just seems different lately," Nicolus said.

"He's gotten used to you—and our relationship, that's all, " Aura explained coolly.

Nicolus couldn't stand it any longer—he moved in for the kill.

"Has a CBT cat ever been interfaced with a computer?"

Swallowing a mouthful of food, Aura unemotionally stated, "The Foundation has never had a need for such a connection."

She was good. Never even flinched. She should have choked. Nicolus smiled as he admired her outer calm, still savoring the tension he had created. It was an orgy of mental torment without a climax—at least not yet.

"Well, time to logon—gotta get that program finished," he said.

\* \* \* \* \* \*

Nicolus worked at the wall unit all day, logging on and off every two hours. He became increasingly frustrated as his concentration slipped away intermittently. He swore and pounded the desk as he continuously failed to understand what exactly was so wrong with the program.

Then he saw it—or rather didn't see what should have been there. He mentally flogged himself. How could I have missed it? It was as obvious as a bagel in a bucket of grits. There was no provision made to abort a "neutral" logon. He had designed the program to deny access to the Network if one or a combination of criteria didn't match, but had failed to write instructions which would deny access if all criteria were absent. Anyone could access the Network if they caught on to this, simply keying in a known passcode, then supplying "white" information to complete the logon process. Nicolus furiously typed in four new lines, disabling forever any possible future neutral logon.

Seeing that his time limit was up, Nicolus logged-off. He sat and tried to mentally assemble a final report for the Foundation. He found it more and more difficult to concentrate, to sequentially arrange the details in his head. He was distracted by the thoughts of Aura's naked body. It had been weeks since he had...the fire, the urgency, returned. He angrily jammed the wrist unit back into his vein and rushed to find Aura. He knew she had done this to him, but he wouldn't let himself ask why. It didn't matter.

Nicolus found her, quiet and alone, going over her pile of data sheets. He unzipped his gown and removed it just as Aura turned to meet his stare with an enticing smile. Aura undressed, and Nicolus took her, unleashing the suppressed passion of the last two weeks. He was lost, completely immersed in Aura. Nothing could matter as much as her.

A shrill whine stabbed at his brain; he wouldn't stop to discover its source. The sound persisted. Aura pushed him away, gasping, "The phone page. Nicolus, you have to answer."

Dressing quickly, Nicolus hurried to the wall unit, breathing heavily, sweat dripping from his forehead locks.

"Please activate view screen," a disembodied voice said.

Thinking fast, Nicolus replied, "The view screen is malfunctioning—please continue."

Lt. General Bailey's voice belched out over the speaker. "Dr. Teal, it is a proud moment for me to announce that you have been chosen to be honored Saturday at sixteen hundred hours at the Foundation's Annual Scientific Achievement Awards Banquet. We congratulate you on your success with the main logon program—and a week ahead of schedule, at that. Impressive."

"Awards?" Nicolus asked stupidly. How did they discover the corrections in the program so fast...without me even writing the report?

"Yes, thank you. Dr. Maitland and I will be in attendance." He signed off.

* * * * * *

"Almost ready?" Nicolus asked, adjusting his tie as he watched Aura squeeze her luscious figure into a tight, blue sequined evening gown.

"These damned tuxedos are miserable. I'm glad I almost never have to wear one," Nicolus said as he yanked at the tight crotch, then pulled an extra half-inch out of the tie constricting his neck.

"It'll take about 30 minutes to get across the park on foot," he said, offering his arm to Aura.

"By foot? Aren't we romantic this evening." Aura was pleased with his suggestion. The sun would be setting soon, and the air would become exhilaratingly cold.

They walked through the bio-cultured grass, enjoying the scenery through their dark-lensed sun shields. The individual black domes seemed to glow pink in the light of Antares. The giant red sun occupied almost seven-eighths of the horizon as it gently began to set in the eastern sky. Giant arms of vermilion and fuchsia star stuff wisped out into space, irretrievably drawn to the white dwarf companion star in a breathtaking dance of celestial seven veils.

The low hum of the automatic hydraulic capillary system that controlled the inside temperature of the huge glass-like city-dome, softly vibrated as Nicolus and Aura walked through the park towards the gigantic central dome. People arrived from all directions by electropod and by foot, appearing as if they were being sucked into the dome by a huge unseen vacuum.

* * * * * *

The auditorium was buzzing with activity as Nicolus and Aura stepped inside. Every scientist in the colony, and at least half of the Foundation Board, was in attendance. Nicolus removed his sun shield and led Aura to an unclaimed table. He sipped sweet ethanol for the hour before the speaker brought the stirring, noisy auditorium to order.

"We all know why we are here tonight," the weasel-faced young man announced. "We are here to honor an esteemed fellow scientist for saving, in record time, our precious Network from certain ruin. Our logon program is now impervious to intrusion or sabotage!" The room filled with a crescendo of applause as the weasel-faced man gestured to Nicolus to join him at the podium.

Nicolus unsteadily made his way through the swamp of chairs and people. Reaching the podium without tripping over anyone, he was greeted by weasel-face offering him a plaque commemorating his success.

Gathering himself, ordering his slightly inebriated brain to attention, he searched for the proper words. Nicolus spoke to the silent, waiting crowd. "I am, quite frankly, surprised that any of my work has warranted such a gracious display of appreciation from my peers. I only did what I had to do: correct my own omissions within the logon program." He paused, lowering his eyes, then continued.

"It is with great concern for my fellow Network users that I must tell you of some of my recent experiences with the wrist unit. I am genuinely concerned that some of the other users may have been affected. But, before I go into that, I'd like to introduce my colleague, Dr. Aura Maitland, without whose support and encouragement, I never would have revised the program." Nicolus smiled subtly as he motioned her to stand.

The audience turned their attention to her as she rose, shyly bowing her head in thanks.

Nicolus continued his speech, elaborating in great detail his experiences with the coma, medication withdrawal, nearly uncontrollable anger, and his ability to logon indiscriminately. He stopped to field questions, readying himself for a deluge of panicked discussion. To his astonishment, nothing happened. He stood there silently staring out into the crowd, waiting. Not one question came.

Flustered, he stepped away from the podium as Lt. General Bailey barged in, taking the microphone in his meaty fist.

"Thank you, Dr. Teal, for your interesting anecdotes. I'm sure we all sympathize with you." He continued to speak, changing the subject completely, vomiting endless paragraphs of political and social propaganda.

"What the hell's the matter with you people—didn't you hear anything I said?" Nicolus exploded, interrupting the Lt. General's long-winded speech. Ignoring him, Lt. General Bailey resumed.

Angry, Nicolus stormed off the stage to rejoin Aura at the table. He guzzled another cup of sweet ethanol, and taking Aura's hand, aimed for the exit.

Wading through the sea of bodies and chairs, Nicolus spotted an old friend in the far corner, near the exit.

"Isn't that Mike Jennings over there?" he asked Aura. Aura had been Jennings' colleague for two years before being assigned to Nicolus.

"Yeah...my God, he's going bald," Aura said under her breath.

"Too many U-turns under the sheets," Nicolus remarked quietly as they slowly inched their way towards Jennings.

"Mike, you fool, how are you? I haven't seen or heard from you in ages. Are you still growing those ghastly plants? I could never eat those things unless they were cooked," Nicolus teased, glad to see his friend. He forgot about the recent fiasco up on stage.

"Still crusading, I see," Jennings said.

"Mike, it's not a crusade. I wanted to make sure no one had been affected as I had, that I got to the logon program before anyone else...."

Nicolus thought hard, looking into Aura's sparkling eyes. He decided to confront her, then and there, right in front of Jennings.

"Aura, what the hell are you doing...to me, to God knows who else?" Nicolus demanded.

"I don't know what you mean, Nicolus."

Jennings interjected, "It's O.K. Aura. Go ahead and tell him. I must say, I'd sure like to hear it all again myself. Your creativity is astounding, Aura."

"Jesus, you're in on it?" Nicolus said, astounded. He directed his attention back to Aura.

"Tell me, Aura. Tell me what the hell you were doing the night before last. I saw you. I saw you with Macedonia, screwing with my medprog. What were you doing? How many other users have you screwed with?" Nicolus was irate.

"First of all—I haven't been messing with anybody's program but yours. I was ordered by the Foundation to do what I did...although not exactly in the way I did it." Aura collected herself, and drew a deep breath.

Nicolus stood, arms crossed over his chest, hands in his armpits, still boiling with indignation, but determined to hear her out.

"Since the Foundation discovered a benign intrusion a year ago, they have been on your ass to get you to revise the logon program. The prospect of having some maniac logon and change all the programs terrified them, but you wouldn't admit it could ever happen. Your repeated refusals made them contact me on the sly. I would either have to convince you, or failing that, resort to chemical 'warfare'—give you the heebie-jeebies—agitate you, drive you to change the program out of pure anger, or even fear. I was originally ordered to dose your food, but that was a problem, because most of the time we aren't in sync.

So I asked the Foundation for permission to alter your wrist unit. They refused, believing it would be too dangerous."

"So what did you do? What were you doing with Macedonia and my medical program? How long has this been going on?" Nicolus demanded, impatiently. The questions kept coming to him. Nicolus tried to file them in his brain, making every effort not to forget.

"I surgically altered Macedonia's Cognitive Binary Translator, adding a parallel interface which allowed me to plug him into the computer. He acted like a 'clean slate', allowing me to logon as anybody I wished...as long as I had their passcode.

"I threw the logon program into a tirade when I tried to use his face the first time; cat faces are arranged similarly to human faces. So, I used a plain white sheet of paper when the face ID came up. I don't know how it worked, but it did. I got into your medical program without a hitch," Aura confessed.

"So does that explain why he keeps staring at me? Is there any possibility he could be reading me?"

"It's possible he picked up lots of things during the logon process. He could be developing neural connections for translating you. Calibration to two people has never been tried...It's quite probable, as a matter of fact." Aura seemed humbled by Nicolus' advanced observations. She stopped speaking, letting him ruminate on what he had learned.

Mike Jennings remarked, "There will probably be an award for you too, Aura. Once this fantastic story leaks out...who knows?"

"Dammit, Aura. You didn't need the cat. That's what was wrong with the logon program; anyone could get into the Network with a neutral logon," Nicolus complained, shifting from foot to foot.

"I didn't know that—I just believed I needed a living body... not me, the Network recognizes me. I followed a hunch and used Macedonia."

"Where in the hell did you learn—such as it is—programming?" Nicolus felt a wave of jealousy and conceit smoke through his whirling brain.

"God, Nicolus. I should have picked up something in the four years I've lived and worked with you," Aura said, almost insulted.

"O.K. Aura, fascinating. What about the sex?" Nicolus dared to reveal this secret to Mike, trusting him.

"That was a kind of 'fringe benefit'," Aura said.

"For who—you or me?"

"Well, I guess, both. I wanted you so bad, Nicolus. I cried

myself to sleep more than once. But you—you and your obstinate determination—your dedication to your work...." Aura's eyes filled with tears as she shook her head and bit her bottom lip.

Nicolus grabbed her by the shoulders, and cautiously shaking her, asked insistently, "What did you do to my medprog—to me, Aura?"

Aura stalled for a few seconds. "I...I ran up your pituitary hormones, which...drove up your testosterone." She stared at Mike's shoes in remorse.

"Jesus, you chemically seduced me? You are shameless, woman, shameless!" Nicolus' tried to conceal a smile, but failed.

"Why testosterone, and not a catecholamine? You would have had the same results—get me pissed enough to rewrite the program."

"Well, not exactly. It was the only way to honor the Foundation's request...and have you in the bargain."

Nicolus stopped his questions, staring directly, coldly into Aura's teary eyes. He consciously controlled his breathing so as not to reveal his confusion of emotions. What a plan. It was fantastic, it was stupendous... it was, all of a sudden, unforgivable.

"What about the coma—why did you do that to me? Did you get off on sentencing me to an eternal void?" Nicolus huffed.

"Nicolus, I didn't do that, at least not on purpose. I miscalculated. I neglected to reset the wrist unit drug delivery system. When you got that flood of luteinizing hormone and testosterone, the delivery system shut down. That's the way we made it; it works in a feed-back loop. In effect, you went into brain shock." Aura seemed apologetic and sincere enough. "I thought I had killed you when I found you there... God, Nicolus, I didn't do it on purpose!"

Jennings listened intently, watching Nicolus for signs of hostility. "You should know about the Foundation's policy on sexual relations between colleagues," he said.

"I do—WE do," Nicolus frowned, glancing at Aura. "I'm scared to death they'll find out."

"Don't worry about it. Do you know how they institute the no-sex rule?"

"I never thought about it. How can they keep people from doing whatever they want in the privacy of their domes?" Nicolus felt like an idiot for never having asked that question, not even to himself.

"When you two wrote the individual medprogs, Aura altered the male and female hormone levels so they would stay way below normal. It was the only way to stabilize the population within this colony, and as a side benefit, efficiency and productivity was increased three-fold.

The men never harass the women; women don't even menstruate here.

"When necessary, mating is chemically encouraged between selected couples. As Chief Medical Officer, Aura is authorized through Special Clearance to make the adjustments in a targeted medical program, routing it back into the wrist unit as a worker is using the Network. Droid workers are simply requested to report to a medical facility." Jennings explained.

"Special Clearance? Is that how I could get into the Network, no matter what I did?" Nicolus asked, completely amazed at Aura's ingenuity. "The Lieutenant General...he knew. He went out of his way to...the test? God, I've been had."

"Exactly. Just more ways to piss you off and convince you to fix the logon program." Aura beamed.

\* \* \* \* \* \*

They walked back to their dome, arm in arm. Nicolus felt an affection, a splendid admiration for Aura. She had tricked him, had used him—but had not abused him. She had elicited the entire spectrum of emotions and made him see every facet of himself. He loved being alive—alive with Aura.

"You wouldn't do anything like this to me again, would you?" he asked.

"No, I...won't be able to. I've been reassigned to dome seventy-five—the senior section. You'll have the place to yourself for awhile."

"Jesus...the senior section. I'll be able to visit you, won't I? It's not over just like that, is it?" Nicolus asked in a spasm of uncertainty.

"Of course we can see each other. I worked too hard to get you. I'm not going to let you get away so easily. After what we've done for the Foundation, they can just stuff their no-sex code."

They walked in the light of four moons, smiling to themselves, enjoying the closeness, the admiration they had for each other.

"Do you think women will always use sex to manipulate men?" Nicolus asked casually.

"Do you think men will always fall for it?" returned Aura.

"I suppose we will. Being four-hundred thirty light years from Earth changes nothing."

www.ingramcontent.com/pod-product-compliance
Lightning Source LLC
Chambersburg PA
CBHW051849170626
46807CB00003B/1405